HARRY DELANEY

UNCHARTED

PX DUKE

Jim Nash Read Order

JIM NASH

Jim Nash The Beginning
Pirate Cay
Thrill Kill Jill
Greetings From Key West
Lost Paradise
No Angels
Mexico Gamble
No Picnic
Fallen Angels
Vendetta
A Girl's Best Friend
Dead End
No Harbor
Dog Days
Startup Blues
Last Stop To Nowhere / The Last
Goodbye
Revenge Is Justice
Escape
Wedding Bell Blues
Snap Brim Fedora Caper
Breakdown
Little Girl Lost
Forget Me Not
All The Glitter
Mexico Time
Partners In Crime
Shop Till You Drop
Lobo
No Free Ride
Gone
Stealing America
Blame It on Djibouti
No Escape
Trouble in Paradise
Nash & Delaney Collide

SEASONAL

Trick or Treat
Helping Santa

JIM NASH INVESTIGATES

The Snap Brim Fedora Caper
The Lady in White
The Lady in Yellow

HARRY DELANEY

UNCHARTED

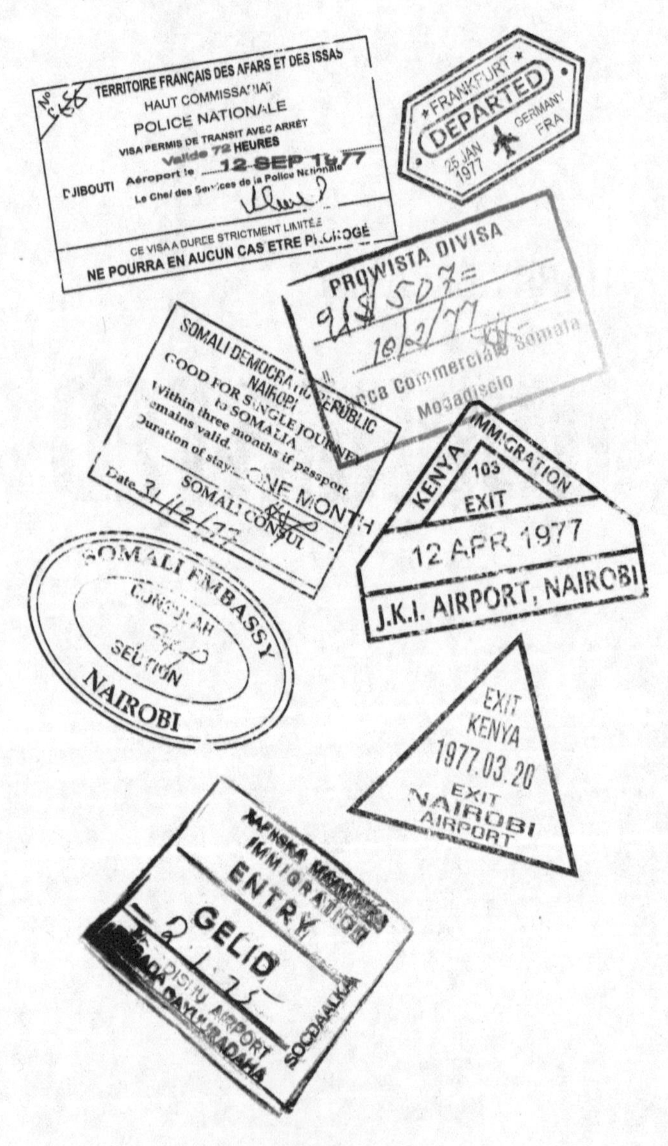
TERRITOIRE FRANÇAIS DES AFARS ET DES ISSAS
HAUT COMMISSARIAT
POLICE NATIONALE
VISA PERMIS DE TRANSIT AVEC ARRÊT
Valide 72 HEURES
DJIBOUTI   Aéroport le   12 SEP 1977
Le Chef des Services de la Police Nationale
CE VISA A DURÉE STRICTMENT LIMITÉE
NE POURRA EN AUCUN CAS ETRE PROROGÉ
FRANKFURT
DEPARTED
25 JAN 1977
GERMANY
FRA
PROWISTA DIVISA
10/2/77
CCB Commercial Somala
Mogadiscio
SOMALI DEMOCRATIC REPUBLIC
NAIROBI
GOOD FOR SINGLE JOURNEY
to SOMALIA
Within three months if passport
remains valid.
Duration of stay   ONE MONTH
SOMALI CONSUL
Date 31/12/77
SOMALI EMBASSY
CONSULAR
SECTION
NAIROBI
KENYA IMMIGRATION
103
EXIT
12 APR 1977
J.K.I. AIRPORT, NAIROBI
EXIT
KENYA
1977.03.20
EXIT
NAIROBI
AIRPORT
XAFIISKA IMMIGRATION
ENTRY
GELID
BADR DAYLIRADAHA
SOCDAALKA

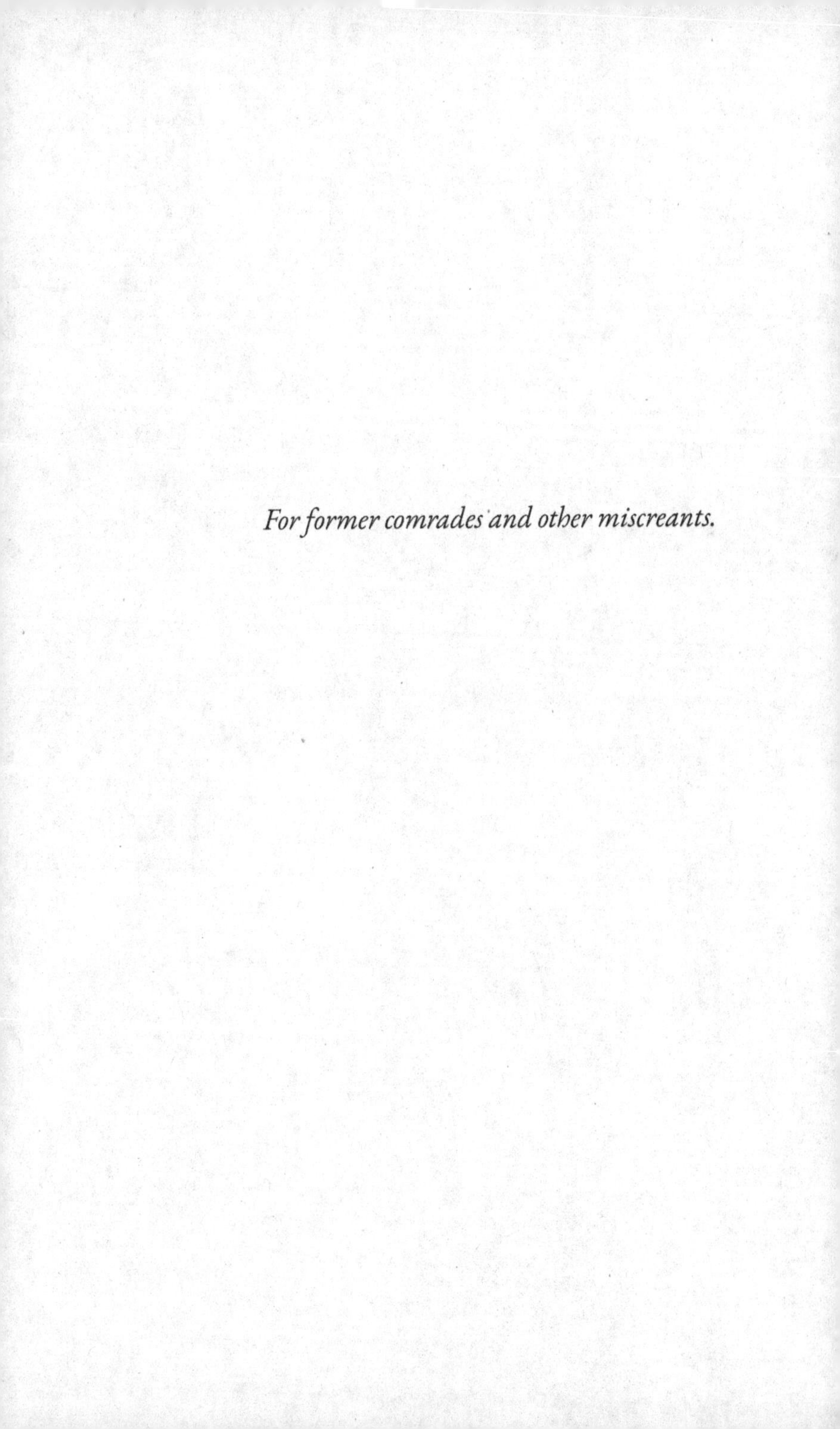

For former comrades and other miscreants.

We were all looking for adventure. Some would say we found it. Others might say we caused it.

Prologue

Harry Delaney leaned over and kissed his wife on the cheek. Satisfied Sasha was still sleeping, he eased his way out of bed. He opened his closet and dug through it for the faded pair of cargo shorts and the old Hawaiian shirt. He put them on and buttoned the shirt. Considering the number of years that had passed, the fit of both was remarkably good.

He made his way downstairs to the kitchen and turned the counter lights on dim. He usually put the coffee on. Instead, he went straight to the garage and a beat-up, old army-green metal ammo box. He slid it off the back of the shelf and took it to the kitchen table.

He inserted a key and unlocked the box. Instead of opening it, he looked off into the distance, remembering. It was so many years ago. He had been younger, on the run from a couple of back-to-back relationships that had gone south. Africa had seemed like the perfect escape at the time, thus he had answered the job ad with a cable.

It surprised him when a return cable arrived, accepting him for the flying job. It was a hell of a deal. When he eventually got the lay of the land, he sent a wire off to his good friend, Mike Williams, to join the party. Mike didn't say no, either.

He smiled, opened the box, and removed the objects carefully wrapped in blue and yellow silk. It had become faded with age.

When might that have happened?

Again he hesitated, remembering as though it were only yesterday.

Kari Nurmi had called the men to attention in the hotel lobby. She watched as they lined up in their squads, with Iván at the head of one and Jofre at the head of the other. She grinned as she stood in front of each man and held up a shirt she had picked out. Each was special for the man in front of her. To a man they had accepted every shirt without complaint.

And why would they complain? Kari was one of them. They had been proud to accept her. She had earned their respect when she stood by in the comms tent when Mike and his squad were under attack.

Harry carefully unfolded the remainder of the silk to reveal the woman's passport. He opened it to her head shot. She looked so young. He hesitated before flipping through the pages covered with visas. A picture slipped out. It was the photo of the men in the cargo hold of the DC-3.

The battle-hardened, tough-as-nails mercenaries wore the colorful Hawaiian shirts that Kari had presented to them. She had told them that if they didn't like what she had picked out, they could trade. Not one man had traded. That each shirt had been Kari's choice was enough.

He set aside the passport and removed the handgun, a French MAC50, still in its canvas holster. The web belt remained wound around it, as it had been presented all those years ago by Captain Renard.

He spread the colored cloth on the table, then laid out the rag and the oil and the bore brush. He uncurled the web belt, flipped open the holster, and removed the handgun. He began stripping it down to its seven components. A noise behind him caused him to halt.

"Dad? What are you doing up so early?"

Christa. As usual, she was checking up on things.

"Oh, I couldn't sleep, so I found something to do."

Stripping and cleaning the handgun had become an occasional ritual, although it had been more than a few years since he had taken it out to check it. This was the first time through the decades he had been caught out.

"Let me finish what I'm doing, please."

Christa dragged a chair beside her father and curled up to observe and learn.

"This once belonged to a very special friend. It was presented—"

He hesitated, unable to go on. His voice caught. He was happy to have something to do. He cleared his throat and finished oiling and wiping and re-assembling the handgun.

"The safety is critical with this particular weapon. If you don't pay attention, in the heat of things—he almost said *heat of battle*—you can flip it on and not realize it."

He demonstrated how it might happen, as he and Kari had been shown by Renard so many years ago.

"Then, in a panic, you'll try to pull the trigger and it won't fire." He put the pistol down on the table beside the box of 9mm cartridges. "In any case, this one has never once been fired."

He replaced the pistol in the holster and fastened the flap. He wound the belt carefully, almost reverently, around the weapon.

"What's that writing on the box, dad?"

"It's French."

He hoped that would satisfy her. Behind him, hands rested on his shoulders.

Sasha. How long has she been standing there?

"What are you two up to down here?"

The sun wasn't yet up. It was only beginning to turn the horizon a dull gray.

"I don't know, Mom. I came downstairs to find Dad sitting at the table."

Sasha took a chair opposite Christa and looked at her husband. "Well? What's up, Harry?" Her eyes moved to take in the steel box and the silk cloth the package rested on. "That's a colorful way to wrap a handgun."

"Yes. It is, isn't it?"

Harry still hadn't looked at his wife.

"Whose passport is that?"

"I think I'll put the coffee on." He moved to stand up.

Sasha, sensing her husband's discomfort, put a hand on his forearm. "I'll do it, dear."

He sighed and settled back in the chair. After all the years, it was time.

"I never told you about the time Mike and I were living in the desert..."

Harry's voice trailed off. The desert had been good to all of them, until it wasn't.

"It was a long time ago. Well before you and I met. We were camped in the sand, with a damn fine crew backing us up..."

1

I happened to be in the comms tent when the call came in over the High Frequency radio. It was Mike Williams, advising his Estimated Time of Arrival. I acknowledged the ETA call and, knowing him the way I did, I made for the airstrip. He would be on the ground in minutes. I wasn't disappointed, mostly because I didn't want to spend time in the hot noon sun, even with the breeze. All a dry wind did was suck away the perspiration meant to cool the body.

Mike handled the DC-3 like he always did. Wheels kissed the sand. Engines went into ground idle immediately. The tail wheel shook, rattled and rolled in the soft sand as though looking for hard ground.

He forced the DC-3 into a brake and throttle turn and rolled to a stop on the sand. No matter how many times we graded the strip, the desert sand never packed down. The vast cloud of red dust kicked up by the engines forcing the turn took its time drifting off in the light breeze. It was the same breeze that brought no real relief from the heat.

The propellers coughed to a halt. Mike stuck his arm out the cockpit window and gestured at the sand. His head followed to take in the expanse he had parked on.

"It all looks the same, Harry. Endless, empty sand as far as the eye can see."

"I'd be careful who you say that to, partner. In these parts, it needs to be translated. On our R&Rs it's a different story with the *wanawake weupe* we hang out with."

"White women are highly overrated, my friend."

That came out of nowhere, but Mike was coming down off a bad deal with his latest girlfriend. Or his latest ex-girlfriend, to be truthful, so I cut him some slack. He was known to have a lot of exes. He ought to be accustomed to it by now. Maybe that was why he preferred to take as many flights as he could. Flying always got him out of the girlfriend blues he found himself in.

On the other hand, while on the subject, I wasn't known as god's gift to women, either.

You could call us even in that department. It was probably one of the many reasons we found ourselves stranded on the Dark Continent for so long. Another reason might be the money. And the camaraderie. The food wasn't bad, either—if we discounted the expense of flying it into camp.

"What surprises did you find for the cook?"

Mike always took along a local crewman when he scored a flight into a town—any town, as far as that went. I, on the other hand, only took my culinary skills, otherwise known as grocery shopping, into the major cities.

He ignored my question. "I need to get Sammy to take a look at the hydraulics on number 2. It was fluctuating like crazy on the approach. Made me glad I was lined up when I noticed."

So much for the briefing on dinner. Mike was supposed to be the part—time backup pilot. He was our chief maintenance engineer. He had help, of course. We had hired Sammy Paulson, an old Africa hand, away from a helicopter company when the lot of them bugged out of Somalia. Mike had agreed to help Sammy out with the DC-3 work.

Like I said, the man needed the distraction.

We were a two-pilot operation. Like me, Mike was qualified on the DC-3 and the Pilatus Porter. Unlike me, he preferred not to fly the Porter. It was always going into short strips with heavy loads. He preferred the security of the DC-3. It might be ancient, his story went, but it fell to the earth only slowly if he lost an engine.

I understood perfectly. The Porter had only one engine, a PT-6 turbine.

The PT-6 was a good engine. It was renowned

for its reliability. It took a lot of abuse and kept on ticking. Which was why I liked the Porter. It made us money getting into those short, isolated desert strips with loads of arms and ammunition and men. The whys and wherefores of the men weren't open to discussion. Neither were the arms.

We had learned to sweat out the Porter's flight idiosyncrasies until we became familiar with it. Getting parts in the middle of a desert wasn't the easiest. Most important of all, we could make it go when it had to go. That was the bottom line when you needed to get things done in this part of the world. Get it done fast, or don't bother doing it at all.

The Porter and the DC-3 gave us flexibility in cargo hauling. It meant we earned our keep by providing services others couldn't, or wouldn't, provide. Things like aerial recon missions over hostile territory. As for Mike, he sometimes liked to keep his feet planted firmly on the ground. He preferred engineering his way through every problem that came up with his usual calm efficiency. He kept us safe with his expert handling and knowledge of the systems and capabilities of both planes.

The balloon tires hanging off of the Porter didn't hurt. That was Mike's modification. Special-built, as he called them. They weren't anything special, though. Just a couple of DC-3 wheels, modified to fit. I was pretty sure we could land on water if we needed to with those things hanging off the landing gear. I hoped we would never need to.

Being there wasn't always easy, but it all gave us purpose during a time when life felt like nothing more than an endless string of hours spent waiting for something to happen. We waited for something more exciting than just another adventure over unknown terrain under dangerous circumstances, where anything could happen at any minute. The *anything could happen* part usually commenced when we got a radio call for an extraction under fire.

We could handle that.

We could also handle the back-haul's pleasant bonus of cash and precious metals. After all, we needed to get paid for our services. *No pay, no play,* was our business credo. We considered getting it painted on the noses of the aircraft. Common sense prevailed when we decided it might be too obvious.

The mercs we worked with appreciated the fresh food we brought in. That was cost—plus. It cost us good money, plus it brought us a well-earned bonus in crew appeal that went straight into the good will part of the account.

We didn't deal with checks. Cheques, either. No matter the spelling, the country of origin, or the number of zeros.

Cash and all we could carry was our deal. And for good reason. We dealt in arms. The highest bidder wins and we collect the gold. We were collecting so much gold that it was beginning to concern us. There were only so many banks we trusted to keep our gold safe.

We paid for the banking privilege, and that privilege was getting expensive.

I interrupted my reminiscing to let Mike know about our latest hire.

"The new engineer is in the city. He wanted a couple of days to pick up some clothes."

Mike looked at me.

"Say what? A couple of days? Didn't wifey pack a bag and load him onto the plane?"

"I have no idea what's going on. I'll take the Porter in later this afternoon. You might as well come. We could use a little time at the Flying Club to catch up on the latest rumors."

It was true. We'd been out in the boondocks of sand and sweat for too long without a break. Our supply flights were up to date. There was nothing lingering that needed our immediate attention. Even the mercs had stopped bitching over the HF radio, thanks to the latest grub resupply.

Ever conscientious, Mike offered to complete the Daily Inspection on the Porter for me.

"Thanks, but you're spoiling me. You can follow up after I do my own DI."

Mike knew how it went. We always did our own, but the offer never went unappreciated.

"What do you think this new guy will be like?"

"I wish I knew, partner. I called some people.

No one had a bad thing to say, other than that he was on the lam from a couple of marriages. They didn't say it was bigamy. They didn't say how many marriages, either, but who knows in this crazy business?"

In the past, unknown to us, we had hired a couple of bigamists. The most recent was a Pole. Ed turned out to have wives from South America all the way to Vancouver Island. He was on the run from all of them. He had quite a story to go along with his latest wife, though. She had started an aviation company on the island and was looking for a manager to help her run it. The company had been a going concern until Ed jumped on board the wife and the company. He always claimed it was his company. After he ran it into the ground, the wife learned too late of his many wives. He needed somewhere to hide from it all.

That somewhere was with us.

Ed had showed up with a suitcase full of pantyhose. The first time he tried checking into a hotel in Djibouti, he opened his bag to reveal the contents to the woman behind the counter. Her reaction was classic.

"No one wears pantyhose in the desert. It's too hot."

Unfortunately for Ed, I was right behind him when he tried playing the big pantyhose wheel to get a room. I waved a handful of cash at the woman and she nodded and allowed us to register.

Pantyhose Ed had a real hate on for me when he realized what I had done, but I didn't care. I paid his wages; he didn't pay mine.

Mike and I had a good laugh over that one. We could never understand why Pantyhose Ed, as we called him from then on, would bring pantyhose into a desert, but whatever. After being turned down too many times, Ed gave up. We never learned what became of his suitcase full of pantyhose.

There was one minor thing Pantyhose Ed forgot to mention when he signed on. It turned out to be the deal breaker once we learned about it. He left out the fact that he was recovering from a heart attack. He wasn't supposed to be flying. Just what our insurance company would like to hear after he suffered an in-air fatal heart attack and piled in one of our airplanes.

While we delighted in his bullshit, it forced us to call Pantyhose Ed's bluff. We fired him on the spot. So much for using us to lie, cheat, steal, hide out, and corner the market on pantyhose. In a desert, no less.

No one waved goodbye.

After that episode, Mike and I decided we needed to be a lot more diligent in our reference checks. And we were, mostly.

We had a replacement for Pantyhose Ed, and we were both heading into the city. While I had a new employee to meet at immigration, Mike had aircraft parts to claim at Customs.

2

Embakasi airport, known as NBO to aviators, was on the southeast edge of Nairobi. It was a fantastic airport. You could see straight through the terminal building from one end to the other. Fans dangled from the high ceiling on long rods. Slow-turning blades barely moved air. I always looked up at this marvel of modern fan engineering and wondered how many decades ago they had set to working, and how many of them had crashed to the floor.

I was late to the gate to witness the landing of the KLM 747 that had arrived some minutes earlier. Already there was a steady stream of passengers disembarking, but our man wasn't one of them.

To be certain, I waited in case he was late off the plane. Then I thought better of wasting my time. I made a beeline for the car and the New Stanley Hotel. I wanted to claim a table at the Thorn Tree Café. It was a popular spot for locals and tourists alike who descended on it all day long.

As luck would have it, Mike beat me to it.

"Don't tell me. He wasn't on the plane."

"Alright. I won't."

I sat down and ordered a drink and then changed my mind. "I'll go check the hotel register."

I slowed on my way past the Thorn Tree, a renowned meeting place for locals and travelers, thanks to Hemingway and the others who made it famous. A bulletin board had replaced the old tree, whereupon weary travelers could pin notes in the hope their missing or misplaced comrades would catch up. The tree was getting a well-deserved break. It was looking a lot better too.

"Bwana Harry."

A huge smile greeted me at the Stanley's front desk. I was a regular at the hotel. Mike too. We liked to stay at the Stanley as often as we could. These days, with the steady increase in tourists and transients, it was becoming almost impossible to book a room on short notice. Youssef, the front desk concierge took care of us as best he could, given the circumstances.

I returned the grin.

"There is a man here who was looking for you yesterday, Bwana Harry. I let him know you would not be here until today."

"Brian with a *y*?"

The man had made it plain on our first phone call.

"*Ndiyo.* Yes. I have checked the register. He has been here three days already. Let me show you."

Youssef gave the book a spin and flipped through the pages. His finger slid down, halted, and there he was. *Brian with a y.*

"He has been checking in with me. The last time he said he would be back in a couple of hours."

Youssef looked at his watch.

"Any time now."

"Thank you, Youssef. I'm in the café at our usual table. If he comes in."

"I will be sure to herd him in your direction."

We laughed, and I made my way back to Mike. Already the man had two women sharing the table. I hesitated, wanting to check them out. Tourists, from the look of it. I didn't recognize the bottle blonde facing me, nor did I expect to. The woman with her back to me—

In between bouts of laughter, Mike introduced Marie and Karita.

"Harry Delaney. Pleased to meet you both."

I held out my hand. Of course. Karita. Karita Nurmi. Or Kari, as I called her. A familiar face from a shared adventure in Dire Dawa not that long ago. Neither of us let on to the others.

We settled in for the long haul while regaling the women with tales of derring-do and life in the desert. It was by an unspoken agreement that we never told more than the minimum. Who would believe us, anyway?

During one of the breaks to order drinks, I overheard Karita speaking fluent Swahili to our waiter. It duly impressed the man. It impressed Mike too. I caught Mike's eye, and he nodded. Several rounds of drinks later, we had lost track of time. Nairobi was at five thousand feet, and cool night air and darkness were descending.

I enjoyed sitting with a view of the rest of the café and its patrons. As best I could, at least, in a place where a tree sat center-stage. The couple four tables away got up to leave. I glanced at Mike. He nodded. I slapped a wad of cash on the table and stood up.

"Ladies, it's time we moved on."

It was only then that the couple returned to retrieve the large bag they had left beneath their table. It was too late. Their forgetfulness had put an end to our outdoor party. It was Mike who asked the question.

"Anyone for the casino?"

The women appeared surprised.

"There's a casino?"

"If you don't want to gamble, there's always dancing at the Madhouse."

That stopped the pair of them.

"How long have you guys been here, anyway?"

I glanced and Mike and shrugged.

I grabbed a quick shower and changed into something less wrinkled before making my way to the mezzanine. The spectacle of Bryn in a tan safari suit brought me up short. Local tailors made them to measure, and measured the man was. Flap pockets and a flat collar. The belted jacket was a bit much, but what the hell. It wasn't my safari suit— not that anyone would ever catch me dead in one.

I checked out his boots. At least they were veldtshoen. As for the rest of the outfit, it was all synthetic. I wondered how long he would last in the desert with that stuff chafing at everything. My thinking was that he went for the no-iron branding since he would have to do his own laundry. The trouble with that thinking was, we had people in camp to do our laundry and make our beds. They swept the tents too. If nothing else, we were organized.

Following introductions, I explained we would head to the casino when the women reappeared. Bryn insisted on telling me all about the place. It gave me an immediate dislike for the man. I didn't let on, and fortunately, the women arrived. My mood altered considerably.

"Sorry we took so long. We're staying at the Intercontinental. We wondered if a couple of single guys would still be waiting."

The pair of them were looking pretty good to a desert bum. By the look on Mike's face, he agreed. Dresses and low heels and only a bit of makeup went a long way with these two. Marie asked Karita why she wasn't wearing the new dress she had bought.

"It's for special occasions only. When I have one, I'll wear it."

Mindful of Kari's Swahili abilities, I made a point of paying attention to her conversations with the locals. Not everyone smiled or grinned broadly when she addressed them in the local dialect, but enough did, and that had my attention. I started grinning too, when she mentioned she needed a job.

"I'm almost broke. Can you help a girl out?"

I knew her from our time in Dire Dawa, of course, but I hadn't let on to Mike. Usually, we didn't keep secrets. I would tell him when the time was right. "I might be able to."

I had already brought up the subject with Mike, but only because of the woman's fluent Swahili. The French didn't hurt either, but I didn't know enough French to test her abilities. I did wonder how she would make out in our desert camp. Amenities were none and bathing was optional.

"Enough talking shop, people. We have places to be and people to see."

The casino was popular with locals and tourists alike. It was small, and crowded too. Mike and I had been coming since forever when we were in Nairobi. Still, there was enough room for us to separate, and I ended up with Karita on my arm.

We marveled at the stiff upper lips and backbones of the British, all decked out in formal attire and gray mustaches. Their women were the same, minus the mustaches, for the most part.

Karita didn't ask too many hard questions. I didn't tell too many lies. I was a firm believer in the adage that if you don't tell lies, you won't make up the wrong thing when you get caught out. It worked for me—most of the time. I kept her busy by asking all the right questions. I laughed when I needed to, and she appeared accepting.

Of course, we already knew each other slightly from Dire Dawa. We had bumped into one another while I was on an R&R. Then things got hot, and I was forced to bug out. I never found out what became of the woman until I bumped into her at the Thorn Tree.

Karita was from Spain via Norway. She spoke French, and of course, Spanish. I had already witnessed her Swahili. In my book, that was a plus, and I resolved to check with Mike one more time to be certain we could find a place for her in our outfit. I laughed out loud when I came up with that, and she asked what that was about.

I didn't explain. There was no sense putting the cart before the horse. Besides, the night was young. We hadn't been to the Madhouse yet. If Karita could survive the Madhouse, she could survive anything, anywhere.

Mike and I walked the women to the Intercontinental, where we kissed them goodnight in the lobby. When the raised-eyebrow glance between the pair ended, we turned and walked away. Considering the long night we had spent dancing and drinking our tired asses off, it didn't take a desert pilot to know we had left the women shocked and confused.

Just the way we like to leave them.

Said neither of us as we pulled open the Intercontinental's lobby doors and beat a hasty retreat to the Stanley.

3

It was barely 0700 when Mike and I met in the Stanley's lobby. We walked out into Nairobi's cool morning sunshine and bright blue sky.

I looked at Mike. "Are you thinking what I'm thinking, Captain Williams?"

"Yes. I do have one question, though."

Mike couldn't fool me. He wanted to know if the woman could cook.

"Let's take a quick cab to the Intercontinental. You can ask when we get there. What are we going to do about her friend?"

"Can she speak Swahili, French, Spanish, and who knows what else?"

"Marie? Are you kidding? It was all I could do to understand her dockside Italian accent."

A little *baksheesh* in the form of a bribe for the Intercontinental's concierge got us Kari's room number. We knocked on her door in stereo. Sounds of a mad scrambling came from behind the door.

"She's stashing someone in a closet."

"Probably."

We knocked louder. The door opened, revealing Kari in her robe.

"What are you two doing here? It's a little early in my day for a threesome."

The quick grin on Mike's face mirrored mine.

"Well, don't stand out there like a couple of desert hillbillies." She opened the door wide and motioned for us to enter. "Get in here."

She locked the door behind us. "Want a drink?

Neither Mike nor I felt the need after last night's debauchery.

"A little water, maybe."

She gestured toward the bathroom. "You know where the tap is.

A smartass. Just what I needed in my life. There was no sense delaying the inevitable with this one. I dived right in. "I don't know what you might remember from last night, but Mike and I, uhh, operate, err, we have—

I looked to Mike for help. He didn't disappoint.

"We have a small operation north of here." He swung an arm and gestured aimlessly.

I felt the need to elaborate. "It's out in the desert."

That was one way of putting it. I raised an eyebrow, but no one noticed. He was doing pretty good so far, even if he was just beginning. I let him go on.

"Harry mentioned you're fluent in Swahili. I

noticed too. Since you're from Spain, I expect you speak Spanish. How's your French?"

We flew into Djibouti from time to time. It was rare, but even so.

Kari looked confused. "My French?"

"Yeah. We sometimes end up in JIB on a whim and a prayer." That was one way of putting it.

"JIB?" She looked even more confused.

"Djibouti. It's north of here." Mike waved that arm again, and looked like he was going to add too, but thought better.

Kari wasn't fooled for even that long. "Guys, I don't know how long you've been wandering about lost in the desert, but Djibouti—JIB, as you so fondly call it—is on the Gulf of Aden."

I was ready to interrupt, but the woman waved a hand dismissively. She got bonus points for that.

Karita paused for effect.

Mike seemed to know better than to interject when the woman was on a roll.

"Furthermore, the Red Sea is in the neighborhood. And—correct me if I'm wrong here—but la Légion étrangère is in the mix too, is it not?"

Well, now. The woman got props for geography. And current affairs.

"Yeah, that could be. But we have one last question."

"Go ahead, boys. Don't hold back on my account."

I took a deep breath. I figured the question needed to come from me. After all, I had been the one to scout her out while we were dancing up a shitstorm last night. "Can you cook?"

She didn't say a word. She walked to the closet, picked up her suitcase and tossed it onto the bed. One by one, she removed her clothes from the hangers and began meticulously folding them before placing them in the bag. She held up a blue and yellow sun dress and looked in the mirror before folding it up for the suitcase. "Why did I waste money on that for a canvas roof in the middle of a desert?"

She sighed, and I took that as a yes.

"There is one more thing we need from you, though."

I got a *Now what* look, but she stopped what she was doing.

"I'll need your passport and birth certificate. And a copy of your visas too, if they aren't stamped in your passport."

"Will I get them back? You guys aren't slave traders, are you? I hear white women go for prime dollars in the Middle East."

"Of course you'll get it all back. It's a mere formality."

I looked at Mike for support, and he nodded. "We just need to verify some things, is all."

She handed the documents over.

"What the hell. I'm only going to live once, right?"

Mike did a fly-by over our camp while I looked for the all-clear signal from our mercs on the ground. I spotted it and flashed Mike a thumbs-up. He banked onto short final for the desert strip. The wheels kissed the sand like they always did when he landed. I pictured the small puffs that would be replaced by the vast cloud when he brake-turned to head down the runway in the opposite direction. Another brake-turn and another cloud, and we were ready for takeoff, in a hurry if need be.

It was always good to have the airplanes ready to go. We liked to park the DC-3 the same way. In fact, it too, was facing the same direction on the shared parking spot.

We pulled down the cockpit blinds, jury-rigged for shade, and joined Karita and Bryn, our engineer and latest hire, in the back. Neither of us had bothered to say a word to them during the flight. We figured on not giving either a chance to talk us into returning to Nairobi.

I opened the cargo door. Hot air flooded the cabin. Red dust followed it, billowing in with the light breeze. "All ashore that's going ashore."

Karita hadn't said a word since we landed.

"I'll have the men set up a tent for you, okay?"

"No need. I'll be sleeping in yours. If you don't like that arrangement, I'll be in Mike's until further notice."

That was good enough for me. The stenciled olive-drab boxes she had been sitting on for the duration of the flight were obscured by the grub order Mike insisted on picking up. I grabbed her bag and helped her down.

"Be careful you don't trip over the tie-downs."

We headed off through the rows of sun-faded and well-used canvas. A wash basin stood beside each tent on a wooden stand.

"They fill the basins every morning, bright and early. Laundry is done daily, pressed and folded. You'll only need one change of clothes. They put the replacements on the foot of the made bed. The tent gets swept out."

I couldn't think of anything else.

"Where are the facilities?"

I pointed at the twin cabanas. One was larger. We had equipped it with a 45-gallon drum for a shower. The drum had been painted a dirty gray.

"We'll put a bar on the door for you. Don't take a shower in the evening. The water gets boiling hot sitting out in the sun all day. At midnight, it's cooled a bit, and by morning it's quite pleasant."

"Good to know. Now, where are the camp women? I need to freshen up."

"I'll introduce you to Ali. He's the camp foreman. He handles everything that has to do with the camp. If something breaks, be it a truck or the water pump or anything else, he's the one you want to talk to."

Kari left me in a cloud of dust in search of Ali. I don't know what transpired between them. The last I saw, he was laughing and leading her to the women. Not long after that sounds of the local women giggling and laughing echoed through the encampment.

"It sounds like she's got the locals on her side. I think we did all right with that one."

Mike wasn't so sure. "Yeah, but can she cook?

Karita returned, decked out in local fare and a shawl. "I had to borrow these. Next trip to town, I have a list of clothes I'm going to need. I don't want to be the white woman in camp looking like an English tramp."

She handed me the list. It was in a script I recognized.

I looked over at Mike. "She writes it too."

Mike had a last question. "Can she cook?

The woman aimed a scalding look at both of us.

I showed her the rest of our camp. I introduced her to the mercs. She reached out to all of them to shake hands.

"The comms tent is next. In plain English, our radio room."

I showed her the setup. Explained the HF radio. Told her there were similar setups in the DC-3 and the Pilatus. She was smart enough to ask about the other radio, and I showed her the VHF and explained that it was good for line-of-sight transmission only.

"Do you keep radio logs?"

That came out of nowhere.

"No. We don't. We don't keep any logs."

"Why not?"

The lunch gong clanged, filling the sudden silence between us. We shuffled our way to the cook tent and ended up last in line. All eyes were on Kari as she approached the table, trying to figure out what exactly was being served. She picked a bit of everything to put on her plate. I was certain she was feeling a strange mix of anxiety and anticipation in the new environment.

"Doesn't look like she's a picky eater."

That got Mike a dirty look for his efforts and a shit-eater crossed his face. "Consider my job done. Is she staying or going?"

Call me a sucker for a woman in need. She was broke and needed the job. "She's staying."

"Good. What are we paying her?"

Kari wasn't shy about that, either. "You will pay me a thousand a month in U.S. dollars. It will transfer into a bank account of my choosing. I'll have one in Nairobi before the end of the month. Thank you very much. Now let's eat."

The others had learned Karita could understand and speak Swahili. A few of the locals began to give us suspicious looks. There was a nagging worry that perhaps Karita's presence had made matters worse. If they caused any trouble, Mike and I needed to be prepared to act fast and get the troublemakers out of camp as soon as possible.

4

Kari spent her first evenings in camp as Mike and I had done on our nights in the desert years ago. She was in one of the lawn chairs. Her head was titled up to take in the overwhelming Southern Cross blazing bright in the sky above.

"I've seen sunsets and sunrises in a lot of places. I've been in desert cities, but I've never been out in the open, free of city lights. I've never seen anything like that."

The brilliant stars sparkled as though they were diamonds. They were beautiful, more so than anything she had witnessed in her travels.

"It's beautiful. I'll never forget it. I do have a question, though. It's about my passport and birth certificate. What did you do with them?"

"Follow me.

I led Kari to our tent and pulled back a part of the canvas floor. I pulled out a box and opened it. "Your original documents are all here if you need them."

"What do you mean, my original documents?"

I pulled out an envelope with the paper I had purchased in Nairobi. "I think it's best that you use these when we're traveling back and forth."

She studied them in the dim camp light. "They look good. Will they pass inspection?"

"Memorize your new name. You were born in Montréal. I gave you that because of your accent. Around these parts, no one will know the difference. Oh, and in case you didn't notice, you're Canadian. Just like Mike."

She examined the passport.

"And you?"

"The same. It's a safe bet around these parts. Safest we've ever known."

I caught myself before saying anything else. She flipped through her visa pages. All of them had been stamped, as the original had been.

"We can't have you holding a passport without visas, now, can we? What do you think of your name?"

She repeated it several times, as though trying to get a feel for it.

"You have the same birthday. We like to keep things simple in the event of a breakdown."

She looked across the tent. "Breakdown?"

"The word was a bad choice." I squirmed only a little.

"How has my performance been so far? Am I doing good? I can operate the radios. I've been keeping the books. The other women seem to think I'm your boss. The mercs are happy with my abilities, even though my abilities appear to include sharing canvas with you."

My living arrangements were not open for discussion with our crew as far as I was concerned, although I'm pretty sure it was talked about.

"It was a lot for you to take in all at once. Everyone appears happy. You are one of our better employees. Dependable. Trustworthy. You don't run off at the mouth. We like you."

"Well then—" She hesitated briefly. "I'd like another five hundred a month for my trouble, s'il vous plaît."

I couldn't say no, but I didn't let on I would say yes, either. No doubt her French was a way of telling me it had become a part of the deal.

Kari had set up a makeshift office in the radio tent. It was where she took over the invoicing. The legal invoicing, that is. Mike and I made sure she never saw the illegal paper—not that we kept any of that. I used it as a fire starter for our evening campfires.

On her very first day, she did an admirable job. Somehow, she had managed to collect all the invoices. She left them in organized piles, ready to go bright and early each morning. It left me wondering how long it would be before she had questions about what she was organizing.

5

Mike **was out** in the DC-3 on a supply run. It would be another milk run, according to what Kari overheard at breakfast. Radio check-ins were to be every 20 minutes.

She had been a quick study when it came to learning about the different radios. VHF stood for very high frequency, which was line-of-sight only. HF or SSB, which she knew to be high frequency and single-side-band, respectively. These terms were interchanged and used for over-the-horizon communications. The capabilities of each. The differences. On-off switches and dials. Squelch controls. Volume meters. Tuning indicators.

She thought she had learned it pretty quickly, thanks to Mike. Harry was a good teacher too, but he got frustrated with her too easily for her liking. Thus, she had shooed him out of the comms tent more than once to let Mike or one of the others take over until they were satisfied with her abilities.

Mike called in via HF with another status

report. She looked at the clock. He was on schedule, and due to be back in camp by lunch. She knew that, because Mike never liked to miss out on lunch. *The best meal of the day,* he had told her on more than one occasion. He never said why. She suspected it was because he liked the noontime soup.

The HF radio crackled. Kari checked her watch. Mike was early. The static coming in with his HF transmission made it difficult to understand. It was droning on over his words. Covering them up.

She cranked up the volume and adjusted the gain, the way one of Harry's men had shown her. It made no difference. It only increased the radio static, making Mike even harder to understand.

She jumped up. The chair tipped and crashed back. Wide-eyed, she understood. Mike's plane was on fire. She gasped. Her heart raced. She shoved the flap out of the way and ran out of the comms tent. Harry would know what to do.

She rushed to his tent. Realized her mistake. Changed course. Headed for the cook tent.

He wasn't there.

She screamed his name and ran from tent to tent. She finally found him in the warehouse. Breathless and scared, she stammered out Mike's last radio call. Tried to explain what she had heard. "Mike is on fire!"

"What?" He looked at her, incredulous.

He doesn't believe me!

"Mike is on fire! His plane is on fire!" She slapped at his shirt.

"That can't be right, Kari. Are you sure?"

She made another grab and began pulling him by his shirt. "Mike called in! His plane is on fire! Hurry up!"

It took a couple of seconds. Mike wasn't on fire. He was *under* fire. Mike was *taking* fire.

"Go back to the tent and listen. If he calls back, tell him we're on our way."

"Do you have a fire extinguisher? He'll need a big one."

Harry looked at Kari like she was nuts. "Kari, Mike is *taking* fire. He's taking *gun*fire. Someone is shooting at them. Get your ass back to comms and let him know I'm on my way with reinforcements."

I left Kari to figure it out for herself and ran for the cook tent. Three mercs were sitting around telling lies over stale coffee. The boredom died instantly when I told them why we had to pick up Mike and the crew.

They and I double-timed it to the supply tent. We wrestled with the setup to get it out to the Porter. I pulled the pins and removed the doors. The crew worked around me, rigging the tripod mount and then the gun. Clevis pins clicked into place. Two crude jury-rigged lengths of tie-down rope prevented the muzzle from aiming at the wing strut or the elevator in the event the door gunner lost track in the heat of battle.

Kari remained off to the side, her hands on her hips, studying us.

I yelled at her. "Get the doors out of the way! I need to get busy!"

She hesitated, unsure.

"Now, woman! Move!"

Three mercs returned with AK-47s and a wooden box. It contained a Browning M2 machine-gun.

Jofre's and Iván's squads were familiar with the idiosyncrasies of the weapon. Sammy, our engineer, had concerns about whether continued use would loosen rivets on our Porter. Mike and I liked it because we could do pylon turns to keep us overtop a target until it was neutralized. It was also known to be reliable. In this business, we all liked reliability, whether it be equipment or men.

The Porter was light on fuel. We tried to keep half tanks, around 600 pounds, on board for just such an eventuality. If I couldn't get to Mike in a timely manner, there would be hell to pay.

I waved to Kari. The engine's slipstream covered her in dust. She shielded her eyes and walked toward the cockpit door. A merc grabbed her roughly by the elbow. It was fine by me. Anything to keep her away from the propeller.

I opened the door and yelled to her. "If Mike calls in again, tell him to go over to 121.5. He'll know what that means."

She walked off with the second cargo door. The merc followed her. I was pretty sure he would tell her about the dangers of being hypnotized by a spinning prop. I hoped he mentioned she should never walk in front of the airplane too.

The last I saw, she was nodding at the man. She began running toward the comms tent.

K ari wasn't sure what she had become a part of. She only knew that once she told Harry about Mike's situation, it was all out. *Balls to the wall*, the guys called it.

She checked the VHF radio frequency dial. Flipped a switch and turned the radio on. A light illuminated the numbers on the dial. She switched it off, then on again, to be sure. She fumbled and searched. The numbers clicked into position until they showed 121.5. She turned the dial and brought it back. The numbers lit up as they changed. She clicked them into place a second time. She found the sound comforting. It felt like she was doing something.

A placard taped above the radio told her she had set the VHF distress frequency. It was the first time she had noticed it.

It was hot inside the tent. She tied both flaps back. Only then did she notice the small cloud of dust. It was drifting away from the landing strip.

Busy with the radios, she hadn't heard Harry take off. Her gaze followed the plane low over a dune until it disappeared from sight.

Harry's radio transmissions came in one-sided with plenty of static. Like Mike's HF radio transmissions. She didn't understand. Harry's voice was steady and determined. Transmissions ceased and then started again. She suspected the gaps were because Mike was replying. She couldn't understand why she couldn't hear him and then remembered VHF was line of sight.

It dawned on her and she gasped. Covered her mouth with a hand. It wasn't static. It was bursts of machine-gun fire. She turned up the volume. That was the background noise. The gun the troops had loaded. The machine-gun.

The sound sent her into a tailspin. The rat-a-tat-tat was coming in over Harry's transmissions. Interspersed was the calm, steady voice continuing to communicate with Mike on the ground. Probably because whoever was firing had to reload. Or something. She didn't know.

Didn't want to know.

All she wanted was for Mike and Harry to come home safe.

She turned around. A small crowd of mercs had gathered behind her. She turned up the volume as far as it would go. Another voice came in over the VHF distress frequency. It matched Harry's, calm and collected.

"You need any help down there, Delaney?"

Karita almost jumped for joy.

Who was that? Was he there to help? She turned to the crowd of onlookers.

They shrugged. They didn't know.

Had Harry called him in? She hadn't heard him asking anyone for help. Harry's radio transmitter switched on. He was laughing. "Not right now, Don. I've got my hands full. I'll let you know in a couple, all right?"

Gunfire sounded in the background over his transmission.

The unknown voice replied one more time.

"Not a problem. If ever I have to come down anywhere, I'll try to make it near your camp."

More laughter, and then Harry's voice came back.

"You better not low and slow. My hands are full. No tour today."

More gunfire. He clicked off, and the other voice came back. "Understood. I don't think the outfit would like to find one of their jumbos in the middle of a pile of sand."

Still more gunfire sounded over Harry's transmission.

"Roger that. Catch you in NBO."

"Good luck, Harry. You and Mike keep safe. 4620 Heavy out."

The DC-3 roared in low over the camp. Kari ran out of the comms tent. Pushed past the crowd gathered outside the comms tent to watch. Changed her mind and ran back in. She looked up, imagining the plane overhead. Safe. She rushed out again, this time determined to get a glimpse.

A bedsheet fluttered in the wind. A black X made a cross from corner to corner. The mercs stretched it out on the ground and placed rocks on the corners.

"What's that?"

"It's safe to land. If they don't see it, they don't land."

She didn't have time to ask more questions. Giant wings waggled. The DC-3 turned and banked to line up for the strip. The wheels kissed the ground with barely a sandy puff. Mike turned on the strip and parked for takeoff. A high-pitched engine whined overhead. Harry.

She sighed, relieved, and rushed back to the comms tent. She picked up a door and made her way to the Porter. A grizzled old merc dodged the machine-gun and jumped to the ground. He made sure she didn't walk toward the still spinning propeller. She handed him the door and went back for the second. By then, the propeller had stopped.

The mercs folded up the bed sheet. Harry and Mike were deep in conversation when she returned. She leaned the door against the fuselage, then retreated to what she hoped would be the relative calm and quiet of the cook tent.

It wasn't so quiet. Or so calm.

The mercs hoisted her on their shoulders and gave her a resounding cheer before dropping her on the table. She wasn't sure what the protocol was, or what the fuss was about. She had only done what she was supposed to do. She did a tame little dance and jumped down.

And that was it. The dinner gong sounded. Men traipsed in. Ate. Yakked. Gave her the look. Made her feel uncomfortable until Harry and Mike sat down beside her.

"You're one of the crew now. Nothing can take that away from you. You did your job with the radios. You stood by until we all got home. The men on the ground know they can depend on you. Let's eat."

Mike leaned over the table in front of Kari. "That's all fine and dandy, Harry, but can she cook?"

6

Kari was in her makeshift office in the comms tent. It allowed her to monitor the radios when the crews were out on a mission. Orderly looking piles of paper littered the top of the desk in front of her. She attempted to push back the chair she was sitting in. Struggled. Remembered there were no wheels on it. She went back to her list. Shuffled some papers. Sighed. Returned to her list. Checked her watch.

It was still early. She was still on a high from yesterday's commotion, and working on her first coffee of the morning. She walked back to Harry's tent looking for a sweater against the desert's cool morning air.

That was when it hit her like a bolt of lightning. She froze in mid-step. It was like someone had switched on a giant floodlight, illuminating the entire scheme. Except the scheme was more like a scam.

She rushed to one of the warehouse tents and

pulled back the flap. Stacks of wooden crates painted an olive drab greeted her. Black stenciled letters and numbers marked the boxes. She picked one. It was too heavy. She found a smaller box. Struggled with the weight. Slid it back and forth to get it into position. She picked up a discarded pry bar. Jammed it between the boards. Nails squeaked. She worked it deeper and leaned on the bar with all her weight.

The top jerked off. She stopped after only one.

It was all she needed.

She shook her head. Of course it was that way. It had to be. There was no other way. The realization hit her like a blind person suddenly seeing light. Why had it taken her so long?

Harry's charm. It wasn't the first time he had charmed her, either.

She returned to the comms tent where she picked up a handful of invoices and set out to find the man responsible. She strode into the cook tent and landed on him. He was choking back stale coffee with two of the mercs. The laughter stopped, and they greeted her warmly after the experience in the comms tent. She returned the smile before slamming down the paper in front of Harry.

She stood, waiting, her hands on her hips, one boot tapping the canvas floor. "When were you going to tell me about this?"

The mercs weren't stupid. They read the room,

made hasty excuses, and found somewhere else to be.

Harry used the opportunity to arrange the sheets of paper into a neat pile before looking up at Kari. "Tell you about what?"

Kari sighed, exasperated. "You're running guns."

Harry reached into his shirt pocket and withdrew a fold of bills. He had counted it out earlier, knowing the question and the conversation was coming. That it was sooner rather than later didn't bother him. "It's payday. Enjoy your newfound riches.

He handed her the fifteen hundred dollars before waving his arm around the cook tent. "And by the way, if you recall, you accepted my invitation in Nairobi after you came running to me complaining about being broke."

It was true. She hadn't thought for a minute about refusing him.

"What happened to all the largess from that job we did back in Dire Dawa in the mid-70s?"

Her foot stopped tapping. "I used that *largess*, as you so politely call it, to get my ass out of there and into Djibouti. If you recall, there was a bit of a—what shall I call it? A bit of a revolution going on? You were front and center, remember?"

She hesitated, remembering her plight. "It forced me to hop onto a train. A couple of hundred others had the same idea. It took us 30 hours to get to Djibouti, thanks to the camels, goats and sheep we hit and killed. It seems the locals like to hold things up until they get paid for their losses. How did you get out?" She waited.

"An old helicopter buddy gave me a lift. Jean-Marc was killed a couple of months later, doing what he loved."

She wasn't expecting to hear that. She knew Jean-Marc. He was a great guy. She had gone out with him for a while. "I'm sorry to hear that. At least you got out too."

"We were both lucky, Kari. You were desperate in Nairobi. It was this job, or beg for enough cash to get a plane ticket home. I would have funded that too. Now here we are." He handed her the invoices.

"What am I supposed to do with these?"

"Pickle jars."

"What?"

"Pickle jars. You know the ones. They're usually sitting on a bar back home. They're filled with pickled eggs."

"Cripes, Harry, but you can be obtuse. Pickle jars?"

"It's the pickle jar theory of accounting."

Kari looked at him, puzzled.

"You take two gigantic pickle jars. Label one *Cash coming in*. You label the other *Cash going out*."

She shook her head and turned to go.

"Hang on. I'm not finished."

She turned back, unsure of what was coming. Knowing it would end up a story.

"As long as there's more in the *Cash coming in* jar, we're ahead of the game."

She held up the paperwork. "I might as well throw these into the campfire.

"That's what I do. I use them to start the evening fire. You want a pickle jar for your pay?"

She pulled the fifteen hundred out of her pocket and waved the paper at a grinning Harry. "I don't think we have a pickle jar small enough. And before I forget, you'd better tell Mike about us. He needs to know we were a thing in Dire Dawa when the crap hit the fan there."

Harry walked out of the cook tent. He looked over his camp. It was too big. Too difficult to move quickly. He had been too soft. That was why the locals liked working for him. He was a fair man who liked to keep the locals happy. Most of the help would have to go. That would take care of the local women. When their men left, they would go with them.

He turned to go back into the tent and addressed Kari. "You know why I brought you here? It's because of the languages you speak. Swahili and Somali for sure. Mike and I can make do, but you're fluent."

"And?"

"French. We're moving closer to Djibouti in the

north. Your Somali is fluent, from what I learned from the locals. We'll need your Somali in the north. There are things we need that we can't get anywhere else."

"And I'm going to help you get them?"

"Yes. If that's all right with you. If it isn't, when we get to Djibouti we'll make sure to get you on the next plane home. You have my word."

Kari pulled the fifteen hundred out of her pocket.

"Well, it appears as though cash is king for now. I'll have to see what comes next month."

She put the cash back in her pocket and skipped out of the tent. She made sure not to let Harry see the huge grin on her face.

7

Sammy **Paulson had** found and isolated the hydraulic problem on the DC-3. Fortunately, he found a spare pump, and he replaced it in jig time. Already Mike was doing the run-up.

It was as good a time as any to corner the man about my previous relationship with Kari. Mike didn't take the news with too many questions. I told him about the difficulties we had run into in Dire Dawa, and he nodded thoughtfully.

"I heard about it through the grapevine, but I didn't know you were there. It sounds like the two of you were lucky. She's definitely an asset, Harry. The languages she's fluent in alone are worth more than whatever you're paying her."

"Fifteen a month, U.S."

"I don't have a problem. We're going to be traveling a lot farther afield soon. We'll need her."

I had to agree, but there was one more thing.

"Before I forget. Kari wandered into the warehouse and opened a crate. She knows we're running guns. She seemed annoyed until I handed over her first payday in cash."

Mike grinned. "Well then. She's one of us for sure. When can I expect my payday?"

I grinned a shit-eater right back. "You'll get one when I do.

Camel caravans passing by our campsite were a regular occurrence. They didn't stray too close, preferring to keep their distance from the unknown. Camels, sheep, and goats paraded in the distance. The people and their animals constantly amazed me.

The first time I witnessed such a spectacle, I knew why the camel was called the ship of the desert. Piled with boxes and canvas bags, their steady gait never faltered.

Sometimes, a caravan would halt in the distance. Ali, our camp foreman, would drive the water truck out and allow them to refill their containers. He often conversed with the clan leader, and would return with news only he comprehended.

I had told him he never needed permission to take them water, or anything else for that matter. Today, the rapid dust kicked up by the returning water truck told me there was something else going on. He screeched to a halt in the dust cloud and hurried up to us.

"Bwana Harry, I have been told about a missing child. She was herding the sheep. She has not returned and—"

I didn't need to be told twice. "Okay."

Mike rushed off to put seats in the Porter and hang the doors.

"Ali, I have to find Kari and explain the situation to her. And I'll chase down a couple of mercs to go with us."

We met in the comms tent where I explained the exercise. The flight would be low-level, perhaps a couple of hundred feet at most. Ali would be in the back with a merc on the other side. Karita would ride shotgun up front.

Ali interrupted.

"No one knows how long the girl has been missing. She went back to look for a favorite lamb that couldn't keep up with the flock. But there are the hyenas and their hunger for errant sheep and goats along the trail."

We glanced at each other. "We'll hope for the best, Ali. We can't do more than that until we spot the girl."

I flew a low-altitude, back-and-forth pattern, east to west. It put the sun in our eyes, then flew the reverse, making it easier to see without squinting and shading our eyes. The trail was well-traveled. It was well-worn in places too. I wondered how many decades and then how many hundreds of years the trail had seen.

The gusting wind buffeted the plane, but additional altitude would make spotting the girl more difficult. I crossed from one side of the trail to the other, hoping for the best. The trail would disappear over hard ground. It would reappear in the sand. Already, the blowing sand was erasing the track in places.

We covered a lot of ground. Covered it again, and then again. As best I could figure, we did the distance a young girl could travel while searching for her lamb. Surely she was not so far off the trail that we would miss her. And surely she would make her way to the trail once she found her precious lamb.

If she was alive.

I piloted the plane closer to camp, still sticking with the desert trail as best I could. I wanted to believe the girl might not be so far from home.

Off in the distance, a cloud of dust was drawing closer. I had noticed it when we arrived on-site. A vehicle, perhaps more than one, making its way toward our camp. Or the camel caravan.

We had been airborne for a good forty minutes. All the while, I was thinking the girl would not last long. No water or hungry hyenas or both would take their toll. Perhaps the wind might be in her favor. It was strong and gusting. Sandy clouds were kicking up. Maybe the low visibility had confused her. Her scent would blow far downwind. That could be a bonus, or perhaps not.

Kari screamed and banged me on the shoulder. The grizzled merc in the back shouted. We had found her.

Ali spoke to Kari in Swahili.

She confirmed he had seen the girl too.

I dialed in more flap and throttled back. The PT-6 hummed, and it appeared to whine contentedly as I lined up on final. The terrain was uneven. Gusting winds had us rocking and rolling. I fought the controls. Ali was lecturing Karita in Swahili over the headset. Occupied as I was with the strong wind and the flight controls, I was too busy to pay attention.

We bumped the ground. The huge tundra tires Mike insisted we install did their job. I hit reverse thrust. The Porter floated on its wheels on top of the field of sand until one wheel bumped gently against the sand-obscured trunk of a long dead tree. We were on a welcome section of hard-pack sand.

I used the throttle to turn and place the Porter's starboard cargo door to face the girl.

She was carrying her lost little lamb in her arms. Certainly, it had to be her favorite.

I smiled at the sight, but the girl was very lucky. Kari shifted in her seat and moved to exit the Porter. I grabbed at her belt to haul her back into the Porter. She gave me a dirty look before I could explain the number one rule about airplanes.

"Never walk around the front of one."

She nodded frantically.

"I understand. Ali already told me."

"The excitement at finding the girl-"

I didn't get to finish. She was off and running to join Ali. He had the lamb in his arms, and everyone was smiling. Kari was busy chattering away and holding onto the girl's hand. I was pretty certain it would be a death grip of happiness on both their parts.

The atmosphere in the Porter was much improved. Our return flight was flawless. The tires kissed the landing strip and we were home. Ali drove the girl back to her family.

Locating the girl and her lamb tinged the campfire chatter with joy later that night. We had done something noble and good. Kari was on a high, elated by our good fortune. I was pretty sure she thought she had found the girl all by herself. She had been the one to spot her, of course. But it had taken a team to find her.

The Southern Cross burned higher and brighter in the night sky for all of us.

8

Ali charged into the cook tent, interrupting our breakfast routine. The rescued girl and her father, the clan leader, were outside. They had something for the woman who had helped to rescue his daughter. Ali motioned for Kari to join him.

She got up and followed him outside.

Mike and I hovered by the door to watch the proceedings.

The girl spoke in a dialect that was too strong and too fast for Kari to fully understand. Ali translated on behalf of the girl.

Kari began by asking the girl's name. She pronounced each word distinctly, as though hearing the language for the first time.

"Bilan. My name is Bilan. This is my father, Diric. What is your name?"

"I am Kari."

The conversation went fast and furious. Occasionally, Kari turned to Ali for help. Even so,

Bilan's father appeared pleased that the white foreigner who had rescued his daughter could converse in some measure in his native tongue.

Kari asked about the lamb, and whether it was the girl's favorite.

She replied, excited to be telling the woman about her pet. Her father's hand rested gently on her shoulder. Finally, he squeezed, and Bilan held out a colorful parcel tied with twine.

"Oh. What is this?"

The girl explained, and again, Ali translated. "It is a *guntiino*.

Kari untied it and held out the colorful material at arm's length. She blushed and whispered to Ali in English. "Are they able to afford such a beautiful dress?

"To turn it down would be an insult."

"Oh, no. I would never turn it down. I accept it with all my heart. Be sure to tell her that."

Ali translated. The little girl blushed.

Kari turned to look at me. She was so proud, she blushed again too. She turned to Ali. "You must ask her to help me put it on. I am not familiar with such an article of clothing."

Ali translated.

The girl looked at her father, and he nodded. She draped the silky material over Kari's shoulder and showed her how to wrap the cloth around her body. When she finished, the girl beamed up at her father.

"Thank you so much, Bilan. I will wear your wonderful gift in the evening, when I look up at the stars in the night sky. I will remember you and your wonderful generosity."

She gestured to Ali, respectful of not touching the man. "Please be sure to translate for me. I want her to understand. When you have finished, I want to bring her into our cooking tent. I am certain her mother will need flour and salt, and perhaps rice and some other things we have too much of to use for ourselves. You must ask what she needs."

After Ali translated for her, Kari led their guests off.

Harry wandered over to the supply tent. He returned with a leather pouch.

Kari had finished with the provisioning. The girl and her father had two rice sacks full of goods to take back to the caravan.

Harry handed over a leather pouch to Kari. "It's for the girl. It's one of our signal mirrors."

Kari addressed the girl. "I have one more thing for you, Bilan." She held out the pouch, then looked at Ali. "Ali, you must explain to the girl how to use this." Kari opened the leather pouch and showed Ali what she had for the girl.

Ali was familiar with the gift. He took the mirror from the pouch and the cloth it was wrapped in and began explaining its use. He made sure the girl understood it was fragile. He pointed out the sight in the middle of the glass, and how it helped to point to wherever she wanted to aim the light. If she wanted to be found, he explained how it would help. Finally, he showed how to wrap the glass in the cloth and store the thick glass in the stiff leather pouch for safekeeping.

When his explanation was finished, Ali agreed to take the pair back to their caravan.

Kari watched them drive off, excited by the morning's welcome change in the camp's dull routine. When the light flashed, she jumped and waved, pleased to no end that Bilan was testing her signal mirror. Then she looked at Harry. "I have to take this beautiful dress off. I don't want to wear it out. You meet the most interesting people, Harry Delaney, and make the most interesting friends. Thank you."

"I'm pretty sure you have a friend for life in Bilan. Friends you can trust are important in this part of the world. I'm pretty sure you can trust Bilan with your life from now on."

9

Kari **recognized the** bright light flashing intermittently. It was coming from where she knew Diric's caravan to be. It had to be Bilan, and she wondered why the caravan had not moved on. She considered ignoring the girl, thinking that she was probably experimenting with the signal mirror. But something—she wasn't sure what—caused her to change her mind.

She went looking for Harry and Ali. Then she reconsidered. Harry would think she was over-thinking what she had seen. Then she changed her mind again. She soon found Harry and Ali. "I'm going to take the Land Rover to see Bilan. They haven't moved from their campsite. It's another opportunity to practice my Somali. I know her dialect is very strong, but that's good. I need the practice."

"Give us a minute, okay?

Harry and Ali moved off and huddled. They whispered back and forth. Ali looked over at her several times. Finally, Harry approached. "I'll go with you. I need to talk to Diric about some things. Are you certain you'll be able to translate?"

Harry headed off to the supply tent while Kari went to change into something more appropriate for meeting with the clan leader and his family. She decided to wear the guntiino. After she changed, she found Harry waiting by the water truck.

He recognized her puzzled look. "It's a desert, my sweet. I thought we might take a little refreshment as a gift. I'm certain it will be welcome."

She climbed in and was confronted by two rifles. The muzzles were aimed at the floor. Three or four magazines with plenty of tape lay beside them. She looked at Harry.

"Oh. Those? Ali probably threw them in. I can't for the life of me figure out why."

She reached for them, intending to take them out.

"What are you doing?"

"You said—"

"Leave them there. I'm sure Ali knows what he's doing. If he doesn't, I do. Now get in."

He pressed the starter and the old truck groaned to life. He steered toward the encampment, driving slowly. The engine continued to groan and complain as they bumped over the rough, uneven terrain. The old truck's water tank sloshed, forcing the truck to list from side to side.

"Why are we going so slow? And why are these guns here? All I wanted to do was take the Land Rover across to visit with Bilan. What's going on?"

Harry ignored her entreaties. "You look very nice wearing Bilan's guntiino. I'm sure she'll be extremely happy to have you visit with her."

He too, had seen the mirror flashes coming from the encampment. He had already discussed it with Mike. Both had agreed that something was going on. Kari's desire to visit was an excuse to show up. He would be welcomed with open arms when he showed up with a water truck in the desert.

"Do you happen to remember the dust clouds we saw from the air during our search for Bilan?"

Kari bumped and rocked in the passenger seat. "I don't recall. I was busy looking for a girl, not a bunch of trucks."

He gestured as he slowed and came to a halt. "It looks like they might be here. I need to know who they are and what they want."

When they reached the caravan, Bilan appeared from between two tents. She looked around carefully before approaching the truck.

Kari smiled down at the girl. "I saw your mirror this morning. I saw your practice yesterday too. Did you see me waving?"

Bilan wrung her hands, a look of worry on her face. "Yes. I saw. I am glad you are here. Some bad men have come to our camp. They have many guns. They came to meet with my father."

Harry reached in for one of the AK-47s Ali had placed in the truck. He withdrew it and seated a magazine before slinging it on his shoulder.

Bilan's eyes widened and she became very serious. She addressed Harry in Somali. "Did you bring the water truck for us?"

Harry recognized *water truck*, and nodded. "Yes I did, young lady. Kari, translate the rest for me, please. My Somali is not up to yours, and definitely not up to Bilan's."

Kari translated, and the girl's look changed to one of gratitude. "Thank you. I will tell my father if he can be interrupted. He is meeting with some people that do not make him happy."

"Perhaps you can tell me what's going on. I saw the dust clouds when we were out searching for you. Are those the trucks? Is there a problem I need to know about? Can I be of help to your father?"

Kari translated.

Bilan nodded. "Haya."

"She wants you to go with her."

"Tell her I will."

Harry waited for Kari to translate, then looked at Kari. "You should stay here for now, Kari. I'll send Bilan to get you if I think it's safe."

She nodded.

"One more thing. If you hear gunfire, start the truck and wait, okay? If I don't show up, get your ass back to camp posthaste and be sure to tell Mike."

He waited for the look he knew was coming. It didn't come.

"Do you understand?"

"Yes. I understand. I am to return to camp without you." Kari harrumphed and turned away to get back into the truck.

Harry knew there was no chance in hell that would happen.

10

Mike Williams **removed** the port-side doors on the Porter. Checked fuel and oil. Saw the mercs occupied in the cargo compartment. They were busy tying down the machine-gun on the tripod. The one thing he always told them to do was to check the restraint ropes.

Those ropes kept the muzzle from being inadvertently aimed at the wing strut or the elevator. He made it a point to never taxi the Porter until he saw those ropes pinned into place. He had even painted the clevis pins a bright red. All four of them.

The Porter's fuel load was good. Six hundred pounds. Half tanks. He had fueled the aircraft himself. He never left it up to the camp workers, though some were more than capable. Harry was the same way.

Satisfied, he checked the gauges. They were zeroed out. He fired up the turbine engine and listened as it settled into a satisfying whine at idle.

He tapped the gauges. It was a habit left over from the old days of piston aircraft. It was meaningless with modern turbines. He did it anyway, taking some personal satisfaction from the action.

Three mercs climbed into the cargo compartment. The Pilatus airframe settled on spreading gear with the added weight. Without looking, he knew they would be stowing their weapons and securing them in the pre-made holders attached to the Porter's airframe. His only concern was the tie-downs for the machine-gun they would clamp into position on its tripod. He did a shoulder check. The red clevis pins stared back.

A merc reached over the seat-back and slapped his shoulder. They were good to go.

Mike advanced the throttle. At the same time, he pictured the three men in the back. They would be arranging cans for the Browning M2 .50-cal door gun. Positioning them just so for a quick change out. The AKs with their *cuernos de chivos*, or goat-horn magazines taped and hanging off the bottom would be secure. He didn't know what the slang term was in Swahili. Or Somali. He didn't care either.

Mike fed in only as much power to the PT-6 turbine as needed to get the Porter airborne. He would keep it in the air the same way. Low and slow. Nice and quiet too.

On liftoff, he made a gentle turn to bring the Porter into wind. It would take them away from camp. He checked the clock and, satisfied, reset power for a leisurely climb. At five thousand feet, he reduced throttle and began leveling out.

The mercs in the back had donned their headsets. One by one, they checked in over the intercom. In the heat of battle, so to speak, they had all learned the hard way that conversing with the doors off and the machine-gun blazing away was impossible. He and Harry had picked up some expensive headsets, complete with spares, to do the job. It allowed them to converse, and more importantly, to hear well enough to know what was going down once the action started.

Mike didn't think they would see action today. Still, it was a good drill for the crew. Mounting the tripod to the floor with the clevis pins. Hanging the machine-gun off the tripod. Hooking up the restraint ropes. Laying out cans and mags and—

Something crashed in the back. He looked over his shoulder, nervous to know what it was. A merc came over the intercom.

"*Pas de problème*, Mike. No problem. It was only an AK come loose. It has been secured."

The venerable AK-47. Some called it the African credit card. Pick it up out of the sand. Haul it out of water. Save it from a mud hole. It never failed to work, and that was why the mercs favored it too. It was reliable. Dependable. And you could get ammunition anywhere.

A merc called in over the intercom, interrupting

his reverie.

"The water truck's in sight. Parked fifty meters from the caravan camp. No one seems to be near it. *Non. Attend.* Wait. Looks like a woman standing in the shade."

"That's probably Kari, you guys. She was wearing Bilan's guntiino when she pulled out of camp with Harry. Is the outfit the right color?"

Mike depended on the guys in back to call out what they were seeing. He and Harry had trained them that way. During the heat of battle, he would be busy flying the Porter. The men took on the responsibility willingly. They were proud to be a dependable part of the team. Essential. That's how Harry had put it to them, and they had agreed.

It was all old hat now. Experienced. Dependable. All a team.

A voice came over the intercom. Jofre, one of the squad leaders.

"Does anyone know anything about those trucks? There's four of them. Looks like one has a machine-gun on the back. Let me put the binocs to it for a minute."

Mike pictured the man raising the binoculars. Fighting the slipstream to get a good look.

"*Oui.* There is a machine-gun mounted on the bed. I think Harry is taking pictures."

A bright light flashed in the cockpit. Bilan and her mirror. She had made them. He imagined the girl smiling up at them, pleased as punch that she had spotted the plane. He waggled the wings ever so slightly. If the girl had good eyesight, she would recognize the motion. If he saw her again, he would ask her about it.

"It looks like Harry is done with the pictures. He's walking back." The man paused. "Okay, Kari is driving the water truck the short distance to Diric's encampment.

Mike ran through the pros and cons of doing a low pass to show off the port side of the Porter and the machine-gun.

On the one hand, it wasn't necessary to show Dirac. He considered them friendlies. On the other, who were the visitors? Would they turn out to be friend, or foe? In this part of the world, it paid to know your enemies. The sooner, the better.

He spoke into the mic on his headset. "I'm going to do a flyby. Don't shoot anyone, okay?"

He chuckled, knowing he had insulted the mercs. When they didn't respond, he knew he was right. He would settle their indignation when he got them back on the ground. A round or two of beer would go a long way in that regard.

He pulled back the throttle and aimed the Porter's nose down directly over the encampment. At the last minute he pulled in power followed by flaps, leveled, and paraded the Porter's port side past the camp and their visitors in a low and slow. "We'll stand off at a distance until our friends get back in the water truck and make for home."

11

Harry spotted it the minute he stepped off the water truck. The truck-mounted machine-gun stood out like an airport beacon at night. He ignored it while he chatted with clan leader Diric and the leader of the men who had arrived in the four trucks. They were negotiating for something. His limited Swahili didn't help, and he regretted his decision to have Kari remain with the water truck.

He waved to her and whistled for her to bring in the truck. While she was doing that, he showed his camera to the truck convoy leader.

The man almost growled and shook his head.

Not wanting to be refused, Harry gestured toward the truck with the gun. He received the okay and was followed by one of the leader's henchmen. The man watched until Harry's camera stopped clicking.

Harry looked up and spotted Mike in the sky. Bilan must have too, because he caught a flash of reflected light on the plane. It only lasted for a split second, but it would be enough to alert Mike. He gave the girl a thumbs up as she replaced the mirror in its leather pouch for safekeeping. "Did you see Mike waggle his wings at you, Bilan?"

She didn't understand him, of course. His Swahili wasn't that good. He thought for a second, and held out his arms. He tipped them as though they were wings, and then pointed up at Mike.

She got it and nodded with delight.

The water truck arrived with Kari at the wheel. As the women went to load their containers, Bilan led Kari off to find her mother. He was certain Bilan's mother would be pleased to see her in the colorful guntiino that the woman and Bilan had gifted her. Kari certainly knew how to deal with people. He was happy he had hired her, and even happier she had accepted after her unpleasant experience in Dire Dawa.

So far, it had been a good day, but he was certain clan leader Diric wasn't happy to have dangerous visitors in his campsite. The machine-gun mounted in the back of the truck was an excellent find. The firepower was junk, but seeing it had given him an idea. He would need a trip to Djibouti to confirm it. Once he did, he would have a much newer weapon to mount in the Porter. If he could lay his hands on one, the new gun would turn the plane into a true flying gunship.

Kari was able to spend time speaking with Diric. She confirmed that the clan leader wasn't happy to have the visitors at his campsite. Finally Harry and Kari said their goodbyes. Kari hugged Bilan. The girl had been so excited to see her in camp.

In the truck, Kari looked at Harry. "He called the men troublemakers, Harry. Did you get that impression?"

"Well, they showed up with that truck and the machine-gun. I recognized a couple of AKs in the cabs. They have firepower, I'll give them that. I offered Diric some protection, for lack of a better word. He thanked me and politely declined. Still, I wouldn't be surprised that he's going to need protection. There is change coming. Oil companies are interested. That means money. Lots of it."

Kari fired up the water truck. Bilan waved, but she looked disappointed.

"What's with Bilan, Kari? She doesn't look happy."

"It's the strangers. She doesn't trust them. Unlike her father, she believes they don't mean well for the clan. She wants to get home safely and away from them. Her father is breaking camp first thing tomorrow."

Harry nodded. "Ah."

Kari smiled. "But she's pretty pleased with her signal mirror. Did you notice she hit Mike with it?

He waved his wings. I checked with her. She saw that too. Smart girl, if you ask me."

Harry had to agree. Her father was no slouch, either. But was he smart enough to stay away from his uninvited guests?

12

Harry knew very well the visit by the armed men to Diric's encampment was a show of force. It was meant to send a message. And it was a message that shouldn't be ignored. Diric, on the other hand, didn't understand—or want to understand. With the oil companies beginning to flood into the region, there was going to be a rush to claim rights. Those rights would be worth countless suitcases of American dollars paid to whomever made the most noise and projected the most strength.

If Diric was forced out of his bargaining position as clan leader, the field would be left wide open to whomever had the power. Or more likely, the firepower. He wasn't certain he should become involved. In any case, it wouldn't be up to him alone to make that decision. He would have to consult with Mike.

Thanks to Bilan, he knew what he would be going up against. She appeared to be the only one who understood what might happen. Thanks to Kari befriending the girl, she had shown herself to be well informed as to the ramifications of allowing the pirates control of the clan's land resource.

If only he could get through to Diric.

At their usual campfire session that evening, he and Mike came up with the plan. It would involve Kari and Bilan, the girl's father permitting, of course. That was the key. The man would have to permit it.

"I don't know what we can do to convince Diric there is danger in ignoring the oil companies and their dollars. I think he's trying to ignore the obvious. Bilan, on the other hand—"

Kari understood too. "Bilan knows. Or at least, she suspects. She has been listening to the other clans when their caravans pass by. A young girl is usually ignored, but with her smarts and her ears, she has been paying attention. She understands her life will change, and probably not for the better."

The trio fell silent as they considered their options.

Harry was first to speak. "What do you think of doing a recon, Kari? Could you convince Diric that you need a guide to cross the desert to the communities to the northwest? Maybe to refresh some of our supplies?"

That rang somewhat true. The camp had provided Diric's caravan with some necessities. Perhaps that would work.

"We can only try. Let's do it."

"No. Let's plan on it. Mike?"

"Twenty-five gallons of water. Twenty of fuel. Fire starter. A flare pistol and flares. Shade and shelter. A handgun, small caliber. Food plus reserve in case the two of you become stranded."

Kari considered. "Bilan is desert born and raised. Are we going to need all that?"

"It's not for her that I'm concerned. It's you. You're not exactly familiar with working or living in a desert—unless there's something you haven't told us." Harry regarded Kari. "Is there?"

"I shall consult with my desert expert when next I see her, all right? In the meantime, get that junker loaded as best you two slackers can. Now then, which one of you weapons experts is going to show me the handgun?"

Mike turned to walk away. "I'm not touching that, Harry. She might take it upon herself to up and shoot me for asking if she can cook."

"Nah. Both Jofre and Iván have been showing her the ropes with the .45. It convinced them to bring out our single .38 just for her."

By the time I finished showing the .38 to Kari, we were both exhausted. It wasn't only the firearm exercise. It was the whole proposal to send Kari and Bilan off on excursion across the desert into the great unknown.

Still, we agreed it had to be done. It would be up to Diric, Bilan's father, to decide whether the girl would accompany Kari. If Bilan wasn't going, there was no way in hell I would let Kari undertake such an escapade all by her lonesome.

I showed her the flare pistol and flares, then demonstrated how to open the pistol and insert a flare. "But remember that if we're not in the area, it will be a long shot if any of us sees a flare."

13

The machine-gun mounted on the back of that half-ton finally woke me up. If one could be mounted on a truck, why couldn't we hang one out the cargo door of our DC-3? I sat down with Mike and tossed the idea at him. He appeared surprised at first, but I could see the wheels turning.

"I admit, what we've got mounted on the Porter is mickey mouse at best. But if we hang something heavier on it, we could end up shaking the airframe apart."

"We need access to firepower, Mike. The only way we can get it is by going airborne. We don't have the manpower to drive armed trucks around the desert everywhere we might need them."

We already had the Porter set up. It had served us well, so far. Sure, the firepower wasn't the greatest, but we could still sling lead out the port cargo door. As to the increased demand for firepower, we could more than likely cure that with a visit to Djibouti when the time was right.

"I'll get back to you on that."

Mike walked off, and I knew exactly where he was headed. Our engineer, Sammy Pollock, would have a huge grin and eyes just as big at the mere suggestion of turning our reliable old DC-3 into a flying gun platform.

We didn't have any equipment close to what could be laid down from a helicopter or a gunship as had been done in Southeast Asia. In any case, there would be no way we could get our hands on something at that scale, especially a helicopter. Even if we could, we'd need ammunition and spare parts. Not to mention the fuel caches spotted everywhere there was a sand dune, thanks to the helicopter's short range.

I followed Mike on his way to see Sammy. If push came to shove, we would leave it to him to come up with something. Sammy had connections in Djibouti, as I had in the past. Eventually, we would be moving farther north and a lot closer to JIB. It would do us good to at least make overtures to those we knew when we arrived.

Next on the agenda was our camp move. The shooting of a dozen clerics in Mogadishu helped speed things up in that regard. When I broached the subject, Mike too, was in favor of changing our location. In fact, in the past, we had insisted on regular moves. It kept prying eyes from thinking they knew our every move, so to speak. As always, the mercs and the locals would be the last to know.

For the mercs, it was simply a matter of loading duffel bags and weapons into the back of the DC-3.

Mike agreed that we needed to trim the number of locals we had in camp. With their women there, it made for a happy camp. Still, when the camel dung hit the fan—if it ever did—it wouldn't be good.

"What do you think our timeline for the move should be, Harry?"

"Just between you and me, we need a trip into NBO first. Probably with Sammy too. I think we can safely leave Bryn here to pick up the slack with the Porter."

"Cripes, Harry. With both of us gone, it's all slack as far as the Porter is concerned. There's no one to put any flight time on it."

"Exactly. I think he's setting us up for trouble. Probably something with gemstones. He was three days early in NBO. Ali at the Stanley told me he was seen in meetings with certain people. Who the hell would he be meeting with if it wasn't something shady?"

There was quite a black market for rubies and other gemstones in this part of the world. Governments tried to put a halt to it, of course, but it went on anyway, like everything else illegal in this world.

Mike was more concerned about Kari and Bilan's scouting party than he was with what may or may not be Bryn's shady dealings. "We can't leave until those two are safely home and out of harm's way, Harry. Neither one of us would ever forgive ourselves if something happened."

I didn't let on that I thought it was at best a hare-brained scheme to be letting two women—well, a woman and a girl—loose in East African desert conditions. Even if one of them was born and bred on the sand.

14

I considered taking our camp boss, Ali, along for our confab with Diric and Bilan. He had proved to be an excellent translator. In the end, I decided against it. Alliances and allegiances in this part of the world were generations in the making. I didn't want to take a chance that Ali might spill the beans, even if he didn't mean to.

I asked Mike to help Kari load the Land Cruiser. I was pretty certain she was tired of hearing my harping about the dangers. No doubt Mike would do the same, but his concerns would be a fresh voice, even if they mirrored my own.

When the complaining was finished and the truck loaded, the three of us retreated to the campfire. Kari was exhausted. Mike was hoarse.

"What did you do to tire the man out, woman?"

She cast an evil look in my direction. "Not a thing. He made me listen all afternoon. I couldn't even take notes. I had to repeat everything. He went over everything three times, at least. Right, Mike?"

Mike was too tired to grin. Instead, he nodded and spoke almost too softly to be heard. "You got it, woman. You'll end up a valuable asset to this outfit yet if Harry and I have anything to do with it. Now then, what did I forget?"

Kari wasn't having it. "We'll be leaving tomorrow." She went off to bed, leaving Mike and me to rehash the scouting excursion.

I did most of the talking while Mike rested his vocal cords. "There's an old Michelin road map in the comms tent, Mike. We should take a look. In fact, we should look to be sure our camp site is marked for her."

That was our final chore of the day before retiring with nervous exhaustion.

Kari tossed and turned and ran through Mike's checklist of what to take more than once. At first, it had annoyed her that he hadn't let her write it all down. Finally, she saw the logic when she began to get it right in her mind.

Unable to sleep, she got out of bed before first light and made her way to the shower while Harry was still asleep. She didn't want him worrying about her. She wanted him to understand that she could take care of herself, no matter the task.

She dressed and left a still-sleeping Harry behind. She shivered in the chilly morning air and returned for a warmer shirt. She had grown accustomed to the cold, acclimatized as she was. Still, it amazed her that a place so hot could be so cold. She checked her bag one last time before making her way to the ancient Land Rover.

She had paid rapt attention yesterday as Mike walked her through provisioning for the desert excursion. Still, she wanted to go over it again for her own satisfaction. It would be good for her to reinforce Mike's instructions.

She partially unloaded each section of the vehicle, placing the items on the sand beside it. In her mind, she went back through Mike's comments.

She made sure to check the tire pressures including the spare. She had the jack, in case of a flat, and some heavy boards for a base in the sand.

Water. There was 20 gallons. Fuel, ten gallons. She wondered if that was enough, considering where she and Bilan would travel overland. The villages weren't far apart, but still, overland travel would increase the demand for fuel since the trails didn't go in straight lines, even across the desert.

She was interrupted by the arrival of Diric and Bilan. They had walked to the camp, and she wondered if Bilan had convinced her father to do so. The girl had a huge smile on her face. She too, was eager to go. Her father, Dirac, was more somber.

Harry and Mike and Ali joined them. They conversed with Diric and Bilan in an attempt to alleviate some of the man's concerns for his daughter.

Bilan shrugged and began helping Kari with the reloading of provisions. The girl's eyes widened when she saw the food Kari was carrying on the vehicle. She spoke slowly so Kari could understand. "You know I will do the cooking and the hunting, do you not?"

Kari looked at Ali for support. He only smiled back at her. "Of course. But I thought you might like to try some of my cooking too. While I am not able to live off the land the way you can, I can cook using spices and flour and make bread and such."

"Bread? My mother has provided *injera*. It will last a long time."

Kari had never heard the word before. She repeated it to be sure.

"Yes. Injera. You will like it. We will have it with all our meals."

"In that case, I can't wait to try it."

"I have walking sticks for us. We will need them."

Kari made sure to place them in the front of the truck. "We will take your father back to the camp. Will he sit in the front or the back?"

"I think he will want the back. It would not look correct for him to be with a strange woman. My mother is understanding of your ways. It is the others in our caravan who are perhaps old-fashioned still."

The women finished repacking the truck. Kari had the compass and the pistol and two magazines tucked into her bag. She made sure neither Bilan nor her father saw them.

Finally, it was time to go. Harry and Mike hovered like a couple of concerned parents. At the last minute, Diric removed a tattered piece of cloth from his bag and laid it on the hood. "Come, daughter, one last time, please. You also, Kari. I must show you the markings."

He spoke slowly for Kari's benefit. Ali waited until the man finished describing each turning point they would encounter in their overland journey, and then Ali translated. When he finished, Kari thanked Diric for trusting her with his daughter.

"I have no concerns. Bilan knows the desert. She knows the routes you must take. We have traveled this way many times."

Diric placed his hand on his daughter's shoulder for emphasis, and she beamed up at him. "I will do justice for our clan, Father."

"I know you will, daughter. Now show me where I will sit. I have not traveled in one of these for a very long time."

Kari lowered her gaze and addressed the man. "Perhaps you would like to ride up front, Diric."

He took time considering, and she thought he might refuse.

"I think I would like that. I will learn if you can drive as well as my daughter can herd a camel. Right, Bilan?"

Bilan beamed. "Of course, father."

The sun had come up. It blazed high in the sky, keeping watch over the vast desert. It was later than she thought. When she first got out of bed, she hoped she would have everything checked over to her satisfaction before they left. That wasn't the case. By her reckoning with the sun, it was getting on to noon, and their journey hadn't yet begun, thanks to her nervous checking of supplies.

Kari started the old Land Cruiser. A cloud of exhaust drifted over them. The wind was picking up. She had hoped to avoid blowing sand and get in as many miles as she could before it began. She tried not to show her disappointment that it would not be so today.

She halted the truck on the edge of Diric's encampment and waited for him to get out. She showed Bilan the flare pistol and told the girl that it must never be aimed at anyone. She showed her how to load it and then aimed it at the sky. "Harry and Mike are waiting for you to tell them we are on our way."

She covered the girl's hand with her own and pulled the trigger on the flare gun. An orange trail arced up into the sky. If the pair of them couldn't see that from their vantage point, they were blind.

Diric's wife had joined him. She nodded to her daughter, and together she and Bilan's father rejoined the caravan.

Harry and Mike made for the cook tent, satisfied that they had seen the flare. It was the sign that the journey had begun. They poured coffee and joined two of the mercs who were on call.

"I'm pretty sure Karita won't be the same woman when she returns, Harry."

"I'm not concerned about that. I'm more worried about what she's going to be setting loose in that girl."

15

Kari **geared down.** The engine groaned. Brakes squealed. The truck bumped and slammed from side to side over the rough ground. Kari fought the huge steering wheel as she rocked in tune with the truck. She tried to steer around the bigger obstacles, only to climb over larger ones. Even in softer sand the engine groaned and struggled when she downshifted and slowed.

The pair had been driving for what seemed like too many hours. Bilan had commented several times that a camel would not be so rough. She thought the girl had enough when she held up her hand.

Kari braked and brought the ancient Land Rover to a standstill. The wind had picked up, and the blowing sand was close to the ground. It was beginning to drift across in front of them.

How long had the sand been drifting? Fighting with the steering wheel and the struggle to keep the rover moving over the rough, rugged terrain had exhausted her to the point that she hadn't noticed. The look of concern on Bilan's face didn't make her happy. Exhausted and hungry, she seemed near panic.

"What is it, Bilan?"

But she knew. In the time since she had stopped, it seemed as though the wind had grown much stronger. They were in the middle of a sandstorm, and it would get a lot worse. Thoughts of being lost and covered in sand came to mind.

Bilan looked at her. "We must find shelter. The wind is too hard. It is going to get much worse. I will walk in front of you. You must follow me in the truck."

Kari worried even more. "Why can't we stop here?"

Why had she asked? She knew the answer.

"The wind is blowing harder. We must not stop. We need to find shelter. You will follow after me in the truck. I will lead you. Come. We must go now. We do not have time to waste. If the wind blows for a day or more we are in trouble."

Bilan got out of the Rover and crossed in front to stand beside Kari. "We will go now."

Nervous and scared for their safety, Kari intensified her grip on the steering wheel. She had to be careful with the clutch and the gas. The last thing she wanted was to bump into Bilan or run her over. Her hands screamed in agony. Her knuckles turned white. Her breath came in gasps.

She released the steering wheel and shook her hands. It didn't help.

She rolled down her window to keep Bilan in sight through the blowing sand. The damned sand. It was everywhere. She adjusted the scarf across her mouth and nose. Tried to tighten it with one hand. It flew loose. She made a grab and pushed in the clutch, halting the truck. She finally got the scarf tightened around her mouth and nose, and her breathing became easier.

She looked up through the windscreen. There was no Bilan. Bilan must not have counted on Kari stopping. She wanted to panic. She leaned on the horn. It only bleated like a sheep. She flicked the lights on and off.

For all of her troubles and worry, she felt a tap on her shoulder. It was Bilan's walking stick. She jumped and almost screamed. Why hadn't she seen her?

"I must walk, Karita. You must follow me. If we get separated, you must stay where you stop, no matter what. If you do not, I will not find you until tomorrow. Maybe later. Maybe never. Do you understand what I tell you?"

She nodded, knowing that Bilan was a child of the desert and confident in her abilities. Kari shook her head at her own shortcomings. She hadn't listened. She would from now on, even if she was exhausted emotionally and physically. This was no walk across a city. It was a struggle for life.

Bilan walked beside the vehicle as Kari drove. Her walking stick moved rhythmically. She gestured with her arm when she wanted to change direction. How did the girl know? How did she know where she was leading them? Where were they going in this blinding sandstorm?

She felt Bilan's taps again on her shoulder. The gesture brought Kari out of her reverie.

Bilan leaned into the Rover through the open window, "We can stop now. The wadi is ahead. You must not drive over the edge. We will walk below the edge. We will have shelter. You must bring food. We cannot hunt until the storm dies. Do not forget your walking stick."

Kari fought against growing panic. The thought of leaving the Land Rover didn't help. It carried all their supplies for the trip. And there was so much to remember. The girl must have recognized the look on her face.

"Do not be concerned. I will help you, Kari. It will be better in the wadi. We will have shelter for many days. And water too."

What about this hunting when the storm died? What would they hunt? What would they use to hunt? There was nothing to hunt in this place.

She tried to turn off her brain. Instead, she found a bag in the back of the Rover and rummaged through it for a tin of spaghetti sauce and a jar of fruit preserves she had grabbed off the shelf in the cook tent. If nothing else, they would have dessert after a satisfying meal of sauce. Realizing she would need to carry the supplies she took the whole bag.

What was she letting herself in for? She should have talked more with Ali about this trip. About the dangers it would present. It was too late now. She was into it. With a young girl. She would trust the girl's abilities in the desert. She would have to. She certainly didn't have any.

"Follow me, Kari. Hold my walking stick."

She rolled up the Rover's window and closed the door.

"The wind will drop when we get below the cliff and into the wadi."

She stumbled after the girl over the unfamiliar terrain. She wasn't walking between tents back in camp. There was only blowing sand in every direction she looked. Wind howled in her ears and drove the sand to bite at her exposed skin. If she took off her scarf, she would end up with a facial. She almost laughed out loud at the thought, but she was too busy trying to blink sand out of her eyes and keep up with Bilan to do more than that. Her grip tightened on the girl's walking stick.

Bilan halted, and Kari bumped against her.

"Do you see it?"

It was all Kari could do to see past her half-shuttered eyelids. She followed Bilan's arm as she pointed out the wadi in front of them. They descended carefully. Wind-driven sand whipped at them. She stumbled and bumped against the girl. Bilan halted. 'It is not far now. You must be patient."

Upon reaching the bottom, Bilan led her toward a rapidly narrowing channel in the wadi. When they reached an overhang, they halted.

"Shelter. I will show you. Did you bring the small shovel?"

Kari shook her head.

"When you are settled, I will go back to the truck and fetch it."

She wasn't sure she wanted to be left alone in the middle of a desert sandstorm. "Are you sure we need it?" Immediately, Kari shut that thought down. If Bilan wanted a shovel, Bilan would have to get the shovel. She was too exhausted to chase after her.

She sat down to wait, too terrified to do more than that. Her heart had slowed. Her breathing approached normal. Even the wind was dying and the sandblasting along with it. It was almost bearable. Almost. Until she stuck her head out from the ledge above.

"I'm glad we are stopped, Bilan. You made a wise decision."

"I know. Stay here. You are safe. Do not move no matter what. If you move, I will have to come and find you. I do not want to be out in this storm. You must wait for me. I will return with the shovel. It will help us to find fresh water."

That was something she could help with. "I have water on the truck."

"We will leave it there. There is water here."

Those words didn't help Kari's state of mind. How could there be water here? In the middle of a desert? In a sandstorm?

Bilan left her and headed off. The girl was only partway up the cliff when she disappeared from sight.

How would Bilan find the truck? How would she know what direction to go to get to it? Kari had no idea where they had left it or in which direction. She only remembered the wind and the sand and how grateful she was to be here, protected. Thanks to Bilan.

The girl was gone for only minutes before Kari began to test the limits of the shelter. She paced the distance across and below the overhang, finding the limit of the wind in all directions. There was plenty of room to stretch out and sleep. Only a fine dust would find them. Bilan had chosen well.

A wadi was supposed to contain water, but only during rainy season. This wasn't rainy season, as far as she knew. The shovel would help. She cursed her forgetfulness for not thinking to add it to her bag of food.

She wanted to investigate the shelter further, but Bilan's admonition to stay put stayed with her. If she had learned anything during the past hours, it was that she knew nothing about this environment.

She was in Bilan's world. She would trust the girl to keep her safe. Perhaps both of them would learn something in the process.

16

The voices were loud and getting louder by the minute. Finally, Harry had enough. He rolled out of his cot and pulled on his pants. Tipped his boots and knocked them together. He hesitated and looked over at Kari's empty cot. Finally, he slipped his feet all the way into the boots in one smooth motion. If there was something inside, it would be crushed. He hoped.

Harry shivered in the cool morning air before splashing cold water on his face. He dried off and donned his shirt. At the next tent, Mike was outside doing the same.

"Any idea what's going on, Mike?"

"Your guess is as good as any."

The commotion was coming from a tent. He recognized the crew that took care of the fuel depot. They were in front of Bryn's tent. An angry mob of fuel handlers surrounded the man. Money. Something about money. And work. Everyone doing the same job. Getting paid to do the same job. That's all his limited Somali could pick up.

"What the hell? It sounds like a revolution in the making. That's the last thing we need, now that Kari isn't here to translate."

He and Mike had talked about her last night. Harry looked at him. "Do you have any idea what this is about?"

Mike had no idea. "I heard money. And job. And work the same. We shouldn't drag Ali into this. If Kari was here to smooth things over—"

But she wasn't. We would need Ali to translate. Since he wasn't anywhere to be found, we figured he was trying to avoid inserting himself into a situation that he might have to deal with after we were long gone.

Mike looked at me. "The cook tent."

I followed Mike into the tent. Ali and the mercs were inside, bent over their coffees, laughing. What the hell? I was pretty sure Ali had to be translating on the fly.

"What's going on? What did Bryn do now?"

The man had been a thorn in our side since his arrival in NBO. In camp, he was causing disruption and breaking up the team. With the fuel depot, no less. Certainly, some fuelers did a better job of it than others, but the job got done. That's all that mattered. There was no reason for an argument that could lead to a fight. Or was there?

Ali turned to us. "The men came to me this morning, before breakfast. Two or three of them are being paid more for doing the same job the others are doing."

Here we go. More money for the same work. That's all they saw. They didn't see that those doing it were doing it more efficiently or were more trustworthy. It was the same job. They wanted to get paid the same. I looked at Mike. He grinned and shrugged.

"Damn it. How are we going to solve this? Ali? Any suggestions?"

"I will talk to my men. It will be up to you to solve the problem with your man."

Ali refused to use Bryn, the man's name. I was pretty certain he had his reasons.

"Agreed. I need to find Sammy. Has anyone seen him?"

I should have known. Sammy was relaxing in the peace and quiet of the comms tent, reading a DC-3 service manual. I explained the problem.

Sammy stood and picked up some tools. "Come with me. I have something to show you."

He led me to the DC-3. Halfway down the interior, he halted. He used a screwdriver to remove fasteners holding down an inspection plate on the floor.

"There are some cable jacks on the other side." He worked the screws out and picked at the plate. It popped off to reveal a small canvas bag.

"What aren't you telling me, Sammy?"

He held out the bag. "Look inside."

I opened it.

Gems. Uncut. Rubies and emeralds, from what I could tell. That was almost certainly prison time in this part of the world. Maybe even a death sentence if the judge was unforgiving of white men stealing a country's future.

"Holy crap! Bryn's been smuggling gemstones? If he gets caught, it's a one-way trip to somewhere none of us want to be." I shook my head, incredulous that the man would put us all at risk. I handed the bag back to Sammy. "Put them back. Is there something you can rig to tell when he comes for them?"

Sammy thought for a moment. "I could probably rig some kind of clapper on an engine cowling. That ought to make enough noise to wake the dead."

"Then do it. And be sure both Mike and I are aware. Thanks, Sammy. That dumb move on his part could cost all of us everything."

Speaking of dumb moves, I returned to the cook tent. The disruption concerning wages had quieted. Money was no longer in the picture, beyond base wages. I was happy. Mike was happy. The fuel crew was happy—which was all we cared about.

I thanked Ali for his efforts on behalf of the camp. We would miss the man and his abilities when we moved farther north.

17

The open desert's freezing morning air hit Kari hard. Wrapped in only a blanket, she shivered uncontrollably. There would be no rolling over and pulling the covers tighter in her cot in Harry's tent. She listened, intent on hearing the wind. She heard nothing and sat up. Yesterday's sandstorm had blown itself out.

She pulled the blanket back over her head and remembered where she was. She raised a corner and peeked out. Bilan was bent over a small fire. She was singing away in a soft voice. Feeling guilty, she stretched, yawned, and crawled out of her bed. Such as it was.

"There is water for washing in the wadi. The other pond is for drinking."

Pond? Just how deep was this wadi? "You have dug up water? I wish you had awakened me. I could have done it."

"There is no wishing. There is doing. It is done."

Kari blushed, thinking how much of a foreigner Bilan must think her to be.

"Do not worry. You will make it up. Breakfast is ready, made with injera my mother has provided. I opened the can of sauce. I hope you do not mind. It tastes very good."

Bilan tore off some of her mother's injera and handed it to Kari.

Kari took it and dipped it into the warm tomato sauce. "Mmm. The bread is excellent, Bilan."

"I hoped you would like the injera. Tonight if we are still in the desert I will cook for us something special. Your sauce will go well."

"That was quite the storm we went through yesterday. Thank you for keeping me safe."

"It is over. We are fine. I saw it coming, but it was too late to do more than that. The wind was strong. I will make sure we do not have another one when we are out in the open."

Kari tore off another strip of warm injera and dipped it into the tomato sauce. She smacked her lips. It was turning out to be just what she needed in her belly after yesterday's long day and the experience of the sandstorm. "I am glad you are here with me, Bilan. If I was alone—"

"If you were alone you would not be here."

Kari blushed again. She knew the girl was right. She needed the girl to survive in the desert. She had no idea how she would repay the girl when this trip was over.

They shared the cleanup duties, and when they were completed, they took turns shaking the sand out of their clothes. Small clouds of dust drifted off down the wadi.

"I am ready. We must go now."

Kari made sure Bilan wasn't looking. She pulled out the automatic pistol from the bottom of her bag. It was still wrapped in leather beneath a soft cloth. It had avoided all the sand she could not. Fortunately, it would not need to be cleaned.

Bilan led the way to the abandoned truck. A thick layer of sand and dust covered it. Inside was the same, but for the windows and doors being closed, it would have been much worse.

"Do you think we could have stayed in the truck, Bilan?"

The girl looked over the Rover. "I do not know about keeping in a truck during a sandstorm. Perhaps we could. If the wind blows for many days I do not want to find out. It is better to have shelter I know."

"I have never seen anything like this, Bilan." The wind had intensified as the night went on. "I hope it will start."

"If it does not, we will walk."

She smiled at the girl's determination. "Should we look at your father's map first?

She hoped the girl would say yes. She wanted her to be sure she knew where they were and where they were going.

Kari busied herself by lifting the hood and propping it open. It was not as bad as she feared. A layer of dust covered the engine. She removed the air filter cover and took the filter out. She tapped it the way Mike had shown her. There was a bit of dust, but no sand. She thought they were lucky, considering the strength of the sandstorm that engulfed them and the time she spent driving through it.

She replaced the filter and closed it off.

"I think we are ready." She reconsidered. Bilan would not tell her she *thought* anything. The truck was ready, or it was not. She corrected herself. "The truck is ready. I am ready."

The girl smiled at her. "Good. Let us go."

Kari turned the key. The truck whined and complained. The engine coughed and turned over and halted. She switched the key to off and twisted it again. The starter engaged. The engine coughed one more time and started.

Yesterday's sandstorm was only a memory. She was thankful for the overnight shelter and the food Bilan had prepared. She would try to do better today. She must not allow Bilan to do all the work.

The desert stretched out in front of them. Already the sun was warming the morning air. They were heading off to confront a very warm day.

The dune hadn't looked so huge from afar. As they got closer, the more formidable it became until it loomed in front of them. It made her feel small in the truck.

"The sand is very loose, Kari. We should go around. The truck will not climb in that sand. We will get stuck."

Kari cranked the wheel and steered to go around.

"It could be very far, Kari."

She stopped the truck, aware that the girl knew what she was talking about.

"Wait here. I will go for a walk. I will be back soon."

Bilan got out of the truck with her staff and her water bottle and the supply bag she had brought. Was she going to desert her? She climbed into the back of the truck and looked off in the direction they had come. She forgot to check the mileage when they started this morning. Regardless, the wadi was certain to be a long way behind them.

"Stay with the truck, Kari. You will be easy to find."

Kari's Swahili was getting better. Even the Somali she had learned in Dire Dawa was returning. Bilan had commented on it last night.

"If you walk away, when the wind comes it will blow over your tracks."

Stay with the truck. And why wouldn't she remain with the truck? Where else could she go?

Bilan began climbing the dune. Each step was slow and measured. The girl sunk into the sand with each step. She made her way to the top, slowly at first, and then more rapidly as the sand appeared to become firmer.

If they could get the truck to the top. It would be simple. All she had to do was start it and put it into gear.

She put it out of her mind. It was not up to her. It would be up to Bilan. Whatever decision the girl made she would follow.

She rummaged in her pack for some of the injera Bilan had insisted she carry. She dipped it into some of the leftover cold spaghetti sauce. Not so bad after all, even cold. Kind of like pizza.

She dug and pushed her staff into the sand and spread her shawl, then dug sand to hold the shawl and the staff. It made a small tent, and she thought she could feel a hot dry whisper of a breeze made by the shade and the sun in the heat.

She would climb the dune the way she had seen Bilan climb. They would have to get over it one way or another. It didn't appear too far to the top. If she got to the edge and saw Bilan, she would make her way back to the truck, where she had been instructed to remain.

What was the harm?

Stay with the truck.

Bilan's parting instruction. She must stay with the truck. No matter what.

18

Harry Delaney climbed into the DC-3's left seat and began going through the pre-start checklist. Sammy Pollard, in the right seat, covered him off. It wasn't Harry's first solo, as he called it, without Mike in one seat or the other, and he was only slightly uncomfortable.

Starting with number one, he fired up the engines, allowing them to warm before taxiing into position for takeoff. He poured on the throttles, released the brakes, and the huge plane bumped down the uneven runway. He was light, and the ancient 3 eased into the air. He smiled, thinking how the Porter would have leaped into the air.

Sammy unfastened his seatbelt and turned around to look into the cargo compartment. Bryn was up from his seat and bent over the inspection hole.

"He's pulling the plate, Harry."

It was just as he thought. The idiot was smuggling. The man had no interest in including the rest of them in his deal, whatever it was. He would get a surprise when he came up empty-handed. "Let me know when he figures it out."

Harry had Sammy replace the gemstones in the bag with various-sized rocks. The man was going to be some disappointed when he found out.

"I think he just stripped a screw."

"No matter. It's worth it to be rid of someone who orders tailor-made safari suits. Does he have his hat?"

"I think I saw him wearing it in the cook tent earlier this morning. He's got the bag. He's not looking in it. He's putting it in his pocket."

Harry let out a sigh of relief. "Let's hope he doesn't figure out what's going on. Don't let him get anywhere near the cockpit until we're on the ground in Nairobi."

M ike sat down next to a squad relaxing in the cook shack. They must have been able to tell something was up by the look on his face. All conversation came to a halt. He briefed them on his plan before they could finish gulping the last of their coffee.

"We're going to be checking on the progress of Kari and Bilan."

The crew didn't appear surprised. Kari had earned a place when she had stood by them in the comms tent until they were safely home.

"We were wondering how long it would be, Mike. The girl is no doubt experienced in the ways of the desert. Even so, I can speak for all of us about our concerns."

"I'm concerned about the gun trucks too. If they're on the prowl, who knows what they might be on the lookout for? We need to arm up. We'll need the door gun too. Better to be safe than wishing for it later."

The squad went into action. They carried their AKs and backups to the Porter. Removed the doors. Mounted the AKs in the carry spots and roped them in. They distributed extra magazines in canvas bags and loaded the cans for the door gun.

With the Porter dressed, as the men called it, they mounted the door gun. They took special care to ensure the lock-out pins and ropes were in place and locked.

Squad leader Jofre found Mike and let him know they were good to go.

Mike nodded. "Ali has heard about a sand storm to the west of us last night. That's the direction the women were headed. We'll have a look-see and be back in time for pie and coffee."

Mike leveled off at five thousand feet and set up for a lazy flight to where he thought the women should be. Twenty minutes went by before a voice came over the intercom. It was Jofre. "I have eyes on a vehicle at the base of a dune, boss."

"Tracks?" Mike asked?

"The tire tracks begin at a wadi. If it was Kari, it looks like they spent the night before heading off this morning."

That made sense. Bilan, an experienced nomad, would seek the closest shelter during a storm. Mike banked and turned the Porter toward the truck and the dune.

"There's some kind of small tent set-up. It's like the ones we see the locals set out during the heat of the day."

"Could it be Bilan? I don't think Kari knows about those."

"Don't know, boss. Wait. There's another one climbing the opposite side of the dune. She's stepping in her own tracks as she climbs."

"That's good. It has to be Bilan. We'll racetrack until we're sure, okay guys?"

Mike got no complaints.

Bilan heard the noise in the sky. She shaded her eyes and squinted against the sun. Her hand went to the leather pouch hanging from her neck and hesitated. Unable to tell who it was, she decided not to flash the mirror. If it was anyone else—

She made her way down the dune to the truck. Kari had made herself a tent against the heat. That was good. The tent wasn't perfect, but it would work. Kari was learning.

Bilan shook the walking stick holding up the shelter. "I will show you how to make a better one later today when we stop for eating."

She pulled two dik-diks from within her robe. "I took only males. We must leave the females to breed."

Kari didn't know what to make of Bilan's efforts. On the one hand, she thought of dik-diks as nothing more than a cute little miniature antelope whenever she had spotted one. They moved very fast and scampered out of sight even faster.

"How did you—" She stopped. She was in Bilan's world. She would never understand the girl's survival instincts or abilities.

"It is time, Kari. We will leave the truck. We will travel on foot until we get to the village."

"Will it be safe here? All our supplies—"

"We will carry only what we need. To carry more would be a burden."

Kari struggled to keep up with Bilan. As the day wore on and the heat intensified, she came to understand that the girl did not need her. She could make better time on her own.

Bilan halted. "We will drink now. When the sun is over there—" She gestured with her arm. "We will halt and make food. I will show you how to make your shelter. Later, when it cools a little bit, we will go on. How are your feet?"

Kari hadn't thought about her feet. She made sure she had thick socks and her well-worn veldtshoen. So far, feet were the least of her concerns. "My feet are fine."

She looked down at Bilan's feet to discover the girl was wearing sandals. Why hadn't she noticed that before?

"I am accustomed. It is good you brought your own proper shoes. I could not wear such things. I will look at your feet when we stop. It is time to go. No more talking."

Bilan led the way.

Kari chased after the girl, stepping, tripping, stumbling, until she got into the rhythm and caught up to the girl.

"Walk ahead of me. I will watch."

That lasted for only a couple of minutes until Bilan caught up.

"Watch me when I walk. Do what I do. It might take you a while. You will learn."

Kari lost track of time until eventually Bilan told her they would be stopping.

Kari almost collapsed in the sand. Nervous exhaustion. It had been the same yesterday when Bilan had led her to the wadi and shelter.

Bilan reached one hand toward her. "Give me your walking stick."

Bilan took it and shoved it into the sand. "These

are long. One must get them deep enough. Now spread your shelter cloth across the top like this." Bilan showed how to do it with her own. In seconds, the girl had her shelter ready. "See? It is easy, is it not?

The girl smiled at her. She didn't want to disappoint such a smile. "Yes. It is easy for you. But I will learn."

"Of course you will. I will be your teacher. You must stay here. I will come back. Do not leave. Do you understand?"

"I will not leave, I promise."

"It is not a promise. You must remain here."

Exhausted, Kari collapsed in the shade of her home-made tent, proud that she could accomplish something, even if Bilan had to show her again. She closed her eyes, and sleep took over. She woke to Bilan poking at her.

"I made food. Do you have injera? We will eat very little and then it will be time to go. We will be in the village soon."

Not soon enough, as far as Kari was concerned.

19

Harry had the DC-3 pointed toward Nairobi. He leaned forward to check the gauges. Tapped a couple. He sat back, satisfied. The flight gave him more time than he needed to think about Kari. He hadn't been honest with her, and it was gnawing at him. Being away from base camp and the men enabled him to reconsider his actions.

He had set Bilan off with her too. A young girl. Born and raised in the ways of the desert. The girl would watch out for Kari while they were in the desert. But still.

He should have asked Mike to take to the air for a look-see. Would Mike do it on his own? Of course he would. Wouldn't he? There were more than enough men sitting around camp. They needed something to do between missions. He considered radioing camp on the single-side-band, the SSB, and then remembered there would be no one in the comms tent to receive the message. Their radio operator was roaming around the desert.

Sammy nudged him from the right seat.

Harry adjusted his headset and uncovered his right ear to listen.

"Bryn has replaced the inspection plate in the floor. He doesn't look real happy. I think he knows he's screwed."

Harry flashed a thumbs-up at Sammy. "He must have opened the bag and looked inside. The contents of that sack will buy us a lot of dry goods. Probably more than we need. They'll help pay wages, too."

Dry goods was the term they used for the boxes of arms. The stencils on the outside of the military-green boxes gave it away, but it made them feel better to call them by another name.

"In that case, don't overdo it. We could always get raided."

"I know. It's not possible to pay off everybody in government these days. There are too many hands out. Speaking of which, these gems should also go a long way to grease some palms."

Harry checked his DME. He replaced his headset and put in a call to Nairobi terminal to amend his arrival time. He used the radio head to switch over to SSB and put in a call to base camp. He cursed silently as he remembered he had dispatched his radio operator to wander in the desert.

If anything happened to that woman, he would

never forgive himself.

"She'll be fine, Harry. The village they're visiting are friendly."

Ali had confirmed that with Diric. Still. There were those men he had run into while checking out Diric's encampment. They weren't overly friendly. They had only begrudgingly allowed him to take pictures of the gun mount in the back of their truck.

He called in distance and direction to NBO. He was cleared straight in. He put in a request to taxi to the fixed base operator. It was approved, and on arrival, he cut the engines and closed the switches. A hangar door slid open. A truck hooked onto the 3's tail wheel and towed it into the cavernous building. The door groaned and slid shut.

Harry was already in the back of the 3. "Bryn. You're fired. Get off my airplane and never come back. Understand?"

Bryn didn't reply. He donned his fedora, picked up his bag, and jumped through the cargo door to the floor of the hangar. He disappeared out a side door.

"Good riddance to bad rubbish, Sammy."

"You'll get no argument from me. He was almost as bad as Pantyhose Ed Godelski."

Harry nodded. "I radioed ahead to get us a pair of rooms at the Stanley. You want to meet up later for a beer?"

"No promises, Harry. I have a ton of work to do

on our dry goods."

Sammy handed the bag of rubies and emeralds over to Harry. He looked Harry in the eye with a steady gaze. "Take care with my wages, my good man. Mike and I and the rest of us depend on you."

Harry looked right back. "Not a problem, Sammy." If there was one thing he had learned about Sammy, it was that he wasn't only concerned about himself. He spread the gems on the floor and pushed half of them aside. "That should cover what we owe for the arms."

Sammy grinned. "I'll try to negotiate. If I don't join you, I'll be here with the product until we can get out and back to camp." He pulled a list from his pocket and consulted it. "Are there any changes I need to know about?"

"More AKs and 7.62 ammo plus extra cans for the Porter's machine-gun. I think I scratched out the old numbers and added the new. We need to get rid of as much of the 7.62 as we can. Someone told me they were going to switch to a 5.62. Personally, I think it's bullshit. We'll get rid of it anyway until we can verify."

"Rumors. There are plenty in this business. If I need anything, I'll leave a message at the hotel. Have a cold one for me, Harry."

"Will do, Sammy. Try to get some sleep."

At the hotel, I asked Ali, the concierge, to send a bucket of ice and a dozen Tusker out to Sammy in the hanger. If nothing else, he could enjoy some lawn-chair ambiance while he waited. I pictured him in front of the huge hangar door, enjoying a beer with a huge smile on his face while the Southern Cross looked down.

20

The city of dust and dreams. It was what Harry called Nairobi from the very beginning, since his first arrival. He used it to provision his desert operation. He smiled, remembering the KLM flight in the back of a noisy DC-9. He was out of London, bound for Amsterdam. He was the only passenger on board. The gate had held the flight for him, since he was a few minutes late checking in. Ever since, he had a soft spot for the airline.

It was a short flight, but the captain had found time to wander back to see what the fuss was about. That's when he had met Don Dewalt. They began trading stories, he of the bush and being a fire pilot, and Don from his early days as a Berlin Airlift pilot. The West Berliners called it the *Air Bridge*. When it was over, Dewalt decided to settle in Frankfurt.

It was an all too brief meeting given the short haul flight, but he had ended up with Don's phone number.

"If you ever need anything, give me a call, Harry."

It would turn out to be a profitable arrangement for both, but he didn't know it at the time. He was on the ground in Amsterdam, and bound for a connecting KLM flight to Nairobi via Frankfurt and his very first arrival in Nairobi. It wouldn't be his last.

The gems were in his shoulder bag, tucked away next to a .45 automatic with a round in the chamber. He could pull back the hammer and be good to go, the devil with the consequences.

That was the last thing he wanted, of course. He would rather unload the gems and make good his escape with enough cash to promise a payday bonus for his two squads out in the desert. They wouldn't get all of it, but they would get a good portion after he split the proceeds with Mike.

Armed as he was, he was still a nervous and easy target in a city as dangerous as Nairobi. Even getting into the wrong taxi could be fatal in this part of the world. It was almost as though the criminal element could sniff out weakness and opportunity. The .45 eliminated weakness. Opportunity would find itself, if he had learned anything about criminal intent.

The evening was unusually hot, and the night was young when he halted at the entrance to the Stanley's bar. He scoped out the customers. Recognized a few old Africa hands. Their numbers were in decline as the hotel looked to more upscale clientele and the higher room rates that went with them. He didn't like it, but the place was comfortable. After so many years, he knew almost everyone who worked there. They had provided him with plenty of help, something he hadn't needed for a while.

Perhaps it was time to move on after all.

He bellied up to the bar, protective of the bag hanging off his shoulder. He made sure to place it against the rail. If anyone was looking for a quick grab, his bag wouldn't be the one they would go for.

He looked around. Checked out the familiar surroundings. Recognized the woman at the other end of the bar. Maria. There was something about her—

Of course. She was an Italian spy, according to Kari. They had only spoken about Maria once, and that was when the subject of Maria's loyalties came up. He was convinced she was a spy too. Kari had eventually thrown cold water on the idea, but since he knew the women to be friends, he wasn't so sure.

She was looking pretty good to an old desert hand too. She was striking with her piercing blue eyes set off by her flaming red hair. The dress was enticing, revealing her curves as it did. But it was her eyes that gave her away. They looked right through him, almost as though he didn't exist. She was focused on his bag. At least, that's how it appeared.

Does she know? How much does she know? Kari hadn't been back to Nairobi since she'd left with him for their camp. Still, she was in the radio room regularly. Perhaps she had used the SSB radio to contact the woman's handlers. If that was possible. Or probable.

He ordered a beer and prepared for a long wait, but it wasn't necessary. Maria approached him. A coterie of hopeful younger men surrounded her. He tipped his glass toward her and took a long drink of cold beer.

It was his job to look nonchalant. He looked over the crowd. The crew he had recognized earlier had disappeared. Obviously off to the greener pastures of the Madhouse.

Lips touched his ear. A low voice purred. "I heard you were in town."

Of course. The jungle telegraph. "Yeah, I had to come in to do some business. We're leaving bright and early."

She appeared surprised. "Is Mike with you?"

"I'm afraid not. He had something in camp that needed to be cleared up."

"What about Kari?"

What about her? And Mike had damned well better be checking up on Kari and Bilan or he'd have the man's hide when he got back.

"I heard a rumor you might have some monkey

business to take care of, Harry. Are the gems with you?"

His jaw almost dropped, and hoped the woman hadn't noticed. Where the hell do these people get their information?

Then it twigged: Bryn. He had to be the source. He hadn't seen the man in the comms tent before their departure, but even so, he could have radioed ahead that he had the gems-until he didn't. "Yeah, I'm afraid Bryn couldn't close the deal. Are you willing to do it on his behalf?"

He didn't mention he had fired the man. He figured he didn't need to if she was at the end of the line for the gems.

Her raised eyebrow gave away the game.

Harry grinned. "With a tic like that, you best not be a poker player. You'll get cleaned out every time. What's it going to be?"

Maria's gaze bored into his. "Who's your supplier?"

Here we go. The third degree.

He thought about telling her it was Bryn himself, but she didn't need to know that. She also didn't need to know that his business didn't rely on stolen gemstones. "You know I can't tell you that, Maria."

He briefly considered giving Bryn up again, but thought better of it. He might need that little nugget of information if things went south.

"When and where do you want to do the

deal?"

She's direct, at least. That's good. "Call my room when you have something for me, Maria. Otherwise—"

He left it open.

Her gaze bored into his again. "Otherwise?"

He didn't look away. "Otherwise don't bother me. I'll be talking to someone who actually wants to buy the product."

If that wasn't obvious enough for her, nothing would be.

Maria turned and made to exit the bar. She turned back to Harry, threw her shoulders back, and took aim with her breasts.

He knew better than to acknowledge her. He had rubies to sell, and Maria's breasts wouldn't have any cash value until he had the cash in his pocket. If nothing else, he was smart enough to know that.

Harry finished his Tusker and returned to his room. He was committed now, thanks to the meeting with Maria. He had no one and nowhere else to unload the gems. He was stuck with Maria, caught in her web of lies and deceit. Perhaps Kari was right after all, and she was a spy. Following their meeting in the bar, he was leaning more toward crook.

And Bryn was a part of the deal. Thank goodness for Sammy's diligent inspections. Without the man, he would still be in the dark about the gems scheme.

He picked up the phone to put in a call to the hangar, but changed his mind. He would take a cab. He wanted to explain to Sammy in person how things were going to go tomorrow.

21

Harry made his way down to the lobby. He signaled for the concierge. Didn't recognize the unfamiliar face. The man's ready smile and the rapid arrival of the taxi, which was a van, alleviated his concern. The VW taxi-vans were becoming popular with tour groups. When back-to-back flight arrivals jammed up the airport, they made hay being available in the city, albeit with raised rates.

He opened the door and climbed into the back, prepared to relax since Maria had arranged to make the exchange. Jewels for money. Why hadn't he and Mike thought of that ages ago? It would have made life so much simpler. After all, what could go wrong? Well, except jail time or execution, the penalties for smuggling protected assets? He tried not to think of either.

There was rustling in the seat behind him. Instinctively his right hand went to cover the Buck 110 in the quick-draw sheath hidden beneath his shirt. He didn't have time for more than that. A cloth hood was pulled over his head and tightened around his neck. He reached for the hood. His hand closed and then everything went black. He had no time to react. No time to object.

So much for trusting Maria. The thought rattled past his frazzled brain as he struggled. Kicked. Waved his arms. It was too late.

Dammit but I should know better by now.

Someone climbed over the seat. A hand on his back pushed him forward. A quick pat-down satisfied his kidnapper. His wrists were bound in front. He was thrown to the floor of the cab. It halted. The door opened. The van tilted twice. At least two more had joined the first.

The van accelerated away.

It would do no good to try to figure out where they were taking him. He wasn't familiar with the city. He would have to depend on chance and circumstance.

One of them would be going through his bag. His .45 would be disappeared. He had the gems in a small pocket. If whoever had ordered him kidnapped, they were sure to still be there.

Harry was certain whoever had ordered his kidnapping wasn't in the van Whoever they were, the men were merely doing a job. That would have been spelled out to prevent screw-ups.

He listened for voices. There were none, not

even congratulations among his kidnappers. So much for trying to figure out who it was. Obviously the concierge was in on it. It wouldn't take much baksheesh to replace the actual concierge with a temporary replacement in any case.

So who was responsible? Maria? Did she want something for nothing? He wouldn't be surprised. Had Bryn thrown in with Maria? Or had he been tossed aside, useless since he hadn't finished the job of getting the gems to whomever was paying him?

So many questions. No answers.

Brakes squealed. The broken-down taxi van slowed, turned, and halted in a short driveway. A gate creaked.

So it's someone with money living behind a walled estate. Of course. Fund the lifestyle with stolen gems and screw everything else.

But he wasn't dead yet. His captors weren't up to the job.

The open gate creaked and banged against something. The van drove past and stopped again. It had to be at the house. Two of the men got out. He wouldn't have much time.

Harry reached beneath his untucked shirt. Found the front of his belt and the sheath off to the side. He used fingertips to slide out the well-oiled Buck 110 knife. It opened without a sound. Clicked almost silently as the blade locked into place. His fingers slid up on the handle and closed. Short sawing motions with the razor-sharp edge did the trick.

His hands were free. He thanked his kidnappers for being the amateurs they were. His hands moved slowly to the hoot. He worked it off slowly. It was difficult to see in the Nairobi night. The van was dark. Street lights weren't a premium, nor were they on this property, wherever he was.

The knee in is back relaxed its pressure. In another minute he'd be dragged out of the van.

He coughed and threw back an elbow. He connected with a quick, powerful jab with all the strength he could muster. The guy's head banged against a window and glass shattered. He found the door latch and pushed. The man slid out, his head hitting the compacted gravel like a melon.

The driver turned to investigate the commotion, but it was too late. Harry was prepared. He pulled the bag down over the driver's head. Tightened the rope. Waited. Tightened some more. The driver struggled. It was fruitless. The man slumped over the steering wheel.

Harry picked up his knife, replaced it in its sheath. He rummaged in the dark for his shoulder bag as he climbed out of the van. His hand located the familiar .45 on the floor. Then he went around to the front, opened the driver's side door. He yanked out the unconscious driver and climbed into the still running van.

He backed past the gate and drove as fast as he could to the hangar and Sammy to check on his progress with loading the DC-3. The arms were more important. The gems would wait.

Sammy had the plane loaded. Fuel on board was sufficient for their destination plus 30 minutes. They were good to go.

"Hang on a minute, Sammy. I need to make a call. Get her pushed outside and start her up. We might need to get going in a hurry."

A night landing with no moon in their flat desert campsite might not be such a good idea. At this point, he didn't care. All he wanted to do was get out of Nairobi with as much material as he could.

He dialed Maria's office from the fixed base operator's hangar.

She picked up immediately. Either she had been waiting anxiously for his call, or someone had clued her in to the missing van and the unlucky occupants.

"Your plan didn't work. I have the gems. If you get cash to the FBO side of Embakasi, I'll be waiting."

He hung up and made his way across the tarmac. Climbed into the back of the idling DC-3. Found a pry bar and opened up a wooden box. AK-47s greeted him. He picked two, grabbed a box of ammo and loaded four magazines. Then he found a roll of tape and began taping the mags together while he made his way to the cockpit.

Sammy spotted the mags and his eyes widened. "You need me for anything? I'll shut her down."

"No. Leave her running. We're going to get out of here in a hurry."

"You got it, boss. What's the deal?"

Headlights turned into the FBO's parking lot. Overhead lights illuminated two people getting out of a car.

"If one of them isn't Maria, we're in trouble, Sammy."

"Maria? Who the hell is Maria? I swear, Harry you and your women—"

Harry clicked a banana mag into his AK, then racked the charging handle.

Sammy did the same.

"Let's go, Sammy. Follow my lead."

"You got it, boss."

Harry relaxed only a little when he saw his visitors were Maria and Bryn. "Look at that, Sammy. Bryn came to reclaim the goodies. If Maria doesn't have the cash, he's broke again."

He called to the pair. "That's far enough. Drop the bag."

Maria answered. "Not until we see the stones. I don't trust you."

"That goes for both of us. Drop the bag and back away. Do it now." He pointed the AK and pulled the trigger. A single round ricocheted off the concrete, kicking up sparks.

Maria dropped the bag and started retracing her steps. Bryn remained where he was. "The stones, Harry. Throw me the stones."

"Not until I see the cash, buddy. I'm sorry, but that's the way it has to be. I'll toss them to you only then."

Bryn followed after Maria.

"Cover me, Sammy. If he so much as makes a move—"

"You got it, boss." Sammy leveled the AK in Bryn's direction.

"Let's go see what we've got." Harry opened the duffel. Rummaged through the contents. Looked up at Sammy and grinned. "I'm just happy to be here."

He heaved the bag of gems over Bryn's head. It landed at Maria's feet. She bent and picked up the bag, then waved it at Bryn. "I've got it!"

A shot rang out. Maria grabbed her stomach and collapsed.

"Shit, he shot her! Empty your magazine into his car. He's not going to get away with this if I have anything to do with it. Cover me until I get to the plane."

Sammy backed to the plane's cargo door. He flipped the AK to full auto and unloaded in the direction of Bryn's car. He hit the magazine release, flipped the mag, and slammed the replacement home. He emptied that too.

Harry handed off his AK. "Don't leave that rifle

for the cops. Throw it aboard and climb in. We're taking off from the taxiway."

"Christ. Are you sure she'll do that?"

"I dunno. We'll find out."

Inside, Sammy slammed the cargo door closed.

Harry made his way to the cockpit. "Take a seat. You're my co-jo. I need flaps now, mister."

Sammy dialed in takeoff flaps before belting in.

"Good job. There'll be a little something extra in your pay envelope next week."

"Glad to hear. I haven't had one of those for a couple of months."

Harry grinned across at him. "Join the club. Mike and I haven't either."

Harry called on the ground frequency and advised he was taking off. He switched to the tower before they could respond. His other hand was busy on the control wheel as he wrestled with the heavy, overloaded plane. The gear bumped and groaned over the uneven ground. Slowly, the heavy plane gained speed until it mushed into the air.

"Gear, Sammy."

The landing gear groaned. Lights illuminated on the panel.

"Two white. We're good to go."

Harry set climb power before calling the tower. He advised them of the body on the tarmac and gave them the shooter's name. "He'll be running around somewhere on the airport grounds. His vehicle has been disabled."

Harry tapped the altimeter and then the rate of climb indicator. The needles didn't budge. He tapped again. "It looks like we're a hundred feet a minute or nothing."

Sammy looked out the window into the darkness. "That should be good enough to get us there."

22

I tidied things up in the cockpit. Adjusted panel brightness on the gauges. Checked the numbers. Reassured myself by tapping a gauge or two with a forefinger just because I could. Satisfied, I turned to look over a shoulder into the darkened cargo hold, then glanced at Sammy in the copilot seat.

"Everything looks good, Sammy."

The man didn't care for night flying. He was forgiven because he was the best engineer we ever had the good fortune of hiring. His Africa credentials were impeccable too.

"You know we had to do it this way, right?"

Sammy looked from front to side window and back. He was more than familiar with the landscape surrounding NBO. He knew we weren't climbing as fast as he'd like. He was constantly checking the gauges in front of him. I told him what he already knew.

"I've got her at full power. I'm doing the best I can."

"Our fuel—"

"I know. We don't have fuel for this. On the other hand, I'd rather burn off fuel than put her down in the middle of the highway beneath us. I reckon we'll clear these hills in another minute or so. Then it's clear sailing to a fuel cache I have stashed just over the Somali border."

That seemed to relax him a little, so I went on. "With two of us I reckon we can hand-bomb enough to get us to camp."

"You left something out, Harry.".

"What's that?"

"It's called dead reckoning, remember?"

"Oh, that. Yeah, I left that part out.

I looked across at him and grinned. "I remember how much you dislike night flying, but consider this. There's no wind. The weather is CAVU. You already know that means ceiling and visibility unlimited. The Southern Cross is taking us to our destination like a radio beacon."

I let that sink in for a minute before I turned the cabin lights down. I craned my neck to find the Cross high above us. "The fuel cache is set up with an approach between two villages. I should be able to pick it out like a winning number on a roulette wheel."

Sammy looked across at me like I was borderline. He had witnessed me at all the Nairobi roulette wheels. It wasn't a pretty picture.

"Relax, Sammy. I trust you to do your job on

this flying tin can. You can trust me to do mine."

That seemed to calm him. I knew it would last only until he heard the power coming back when I lined up in the dark to land at the fuel cache. I leaned forward to confirm it was still a star-lit night.

"The town we're making for is Dhobley. It's just inside the Somali border with Kenya. We'll be over the road most of the way."

That took care of it for Sammy. He pushed the seat back, stretched out as best he could, and closed the only eye that I could see. I suspected he kept his other eye peeled to look out the starboard window. I wouldn't pretend to wake him until I needed those eyes later in the night.

I ran over the panel. The numbers were normal. I reached to tap a couple of them. The readings didn't change. I wasn't taking any chances with the old girl's engines. She had proven reliable in the past. Today was a new day. I checked again, and that was when my eyes fell on the clock. I checked the time against the chronometer on my wrist.

Should I wake Sammy to let him know?

I looked across at him, maybe fast asleep, and thought better of it. He'd be in a much better frame of mind when I gave him the news after the engine alarm clock woke him up. The power dialing back was all it would take.

I eased back the throttles. Sammy was one of those old-time aircraft engineers who kept an ear on things even when he was fast asleep. I knew I was right when he stretched and bumped his forehead against the side window. "We must he there. Holy crap."

We would be landing at Dhobley into the rising sun. Twilight brightened the horizon, but the purple line wasn't enough for sunrise yet. I called for gear. Sammy snapped into action. He nudged the selector. I listened for the sound. He did too, and then called it.

"Two green."

I flicked my eyes to check his work. I kept power on and floated above the sand until I crossed the threshold. I pulled back and the old girl settled like I knew what I was doing. Hello Dhobley.

I braked and slowed before turning to taxi to the approach end of the sand runway. I turned again and cut the engines.

Sammy got up and went back to open the cargo door. Dust and cold air blew in.

"We should have some trucks loaded with 45-gallon drums coming along shortly. They'll have a gasoline engine to help us out. Don't shoot them."

"I was just about to ask. Vehicles are coming up," he announced.

I followed Sammy out the door to be greeted by an old friend. Yuusuf and his family were paid for his constant attention listening for the familiar DC-3. They were happy for the money.

"Jambo. Good to see you, Yuusuf. Hibari? How are you?"

"Mazuri. I am well. I wondered if I would be seeing you again."

"I'm afraid this will be the last time. We must move farther north. I will be forced to deal with Djibouti."

"In that case, how is your Somali?"

"Not so good, but my French isn't too bad. I managed to come up with what I hope will be payment for this unscheduled trip. I hope it will be enough for your family."

Yuusuf looked after several brothers and cousins in this barren part of the world. The village didn't provide much opportunity for work, and his provisioning of my airplane paid for a lot of family. "We will get by. Inshallah. God willing."

Already Yuusuf's crew had the ladder leaning against the wing. Two men climbed up and hoisted the fueling hose. The gasoline-powered pump started and hummed. The fueler squeezed the nozzle. Fuel streamed to the ground, flushing sand and dust out of the nozzle. Sammy nervously oversaw the operation.

"Your men work well, Yuusuf."

I reached into a pocket and was reassured by what I felt there. "I hope I can make up for the lost business, my friend. I want your family to be rewarded for your hard work in helping out our business."

"How is Mike?

"He too is well. He's holding down the fort back in camp. I will be seeing him shortly. Do you have family in Djibouti?"

"No, my friend. It is not a part of my world. Nor do I want it to be."

I pulled my hand from the pocket and handed him a stash of dollars.

Yuusuf's eyes went wide.

"That is for all of your help. Without you, we wouldn't be able to do what we do."

I thought it fortunate that Yuusuf didn't know what we did. Nor did he ever ask. I never allowed him or his men to get close to the cargo door, and it was always closed tightly when we were on the ground.

Sammy concentrated on getting the five-gallon pails of oil into the back of the airplane. He needed to refill the 55-gallon drum of oil he had stored up front. It had been rigged to feed the engines with oil in flight. It was one of the reasons we hired Sammy. His engineering abilities were unprecedented.

Yuusuf and his crew finished the fueling. I thanked him a final time, and handed him a little extra cash for the police chief.

"Tell him we had nothing to declare."

The comforts of our desert camp would be

coming up. I was anxious to find out what was going on with Kari and Bilan.

I positioned the DC-3 and stood on the brakes while advancing throttles. I sensed Sammy's concern in the co-pilot's seat.

"Not a problem, my good man. If it all goes to hell in a hand-basket, we have the sand to cushion the landing."

It was a long takeoff roll into the rising sun. We bumped and listed over the unprepared airstrip. The engines roared. I pulled back on the column. One last look at the instruments and we were climbing out.

With my hands finally free and at altitude, I tried calling base camp on the high frequency SSB. I wasn't able to raise anyone.

23

Bilan slowed. Kari slowed with her. The girl gestured.

"Keep walking."

"What are you doing? Why are you stopping? Are we quitting? We can't quit."

The girl caught up to her, finally. "I only wanted to see you walk. There are many ways. It depends on the sand and how flat the ground is and if there are rocks and if it is hard ground or soft."

Relieved, Kari kept going. "I am trying to learn. You are a good teacher, I think." Immediately Kari remembered there was no thinking with this girl. You either did, or you did not, according to her.

Bilan was not flattered by Kari's compliment. She was too practical. "You are getting better. It will take time. Your feet are going to need rest eventually. You are not accustomed to the sand. Or what you are wearing on your feet."

It was evident that she would be no match for Bilan if they had to do a long-distance trek across the sand. The girl's thirteen or fourteen years of living in the desert had much to do with it. Still, she kept going, wanting more encouragement from the girl. "I'm not so certain I am getting better. My feet are sore and I am tired."

Bilan kept looking forward. "Practice is good, Kari."

They had been forced to abandon the truck at the foot of a massive dune blocking their way. The sand was soft. The heavy truck would sink to the axles. If she allowed that to happen, there would be no way they could get back to their camps without a very long walk.

Bilan passed her and halted. She looked up at the sky, and then down at her shadow. "We stop now. We will drink. We will eat a little food. We will put up our shelter and then we will sleep."

Easy for the girl to say, but Kari said nothing. She needed the rest. She suspected Bilan needed no rest at all.

"Your Swahili is getting better too, Kari. You must have a good teacher." The girl smiled at her.

"I have the best teacher for everything in the desert, Bilan. That teacher is you. I will never forget this adventure as long as I live."

"Inshallah."

Kari repeated Bilan's invocation. "Inshallah."

Bilan helped her dig and push the walking stick into the sand. She laid out the shawl and scooped sand around the edges to hold it down. When she finished, it ended up a shelter to provide shade and protection against the sun and the heat. "I will make a small fire with camel dung. You will watch how I do it."

"Camel dung? I see only scattered rocks."

They looked like rocks to her. She had dismissed them outright.

Bilan grinned. "If that is so, you will help me to gather the rocks."

The girl had the fire going in minutes. They washed their hands. Soon they were enjoying the leftover dik-dik.

Kari showed the girl how to wrap the meat with her mother's injera. She added a bit of the tomato sauce before closing the ends of the wrap. "That is how they eat some things in Mexico.

Bilan looked at her quizzically. Of course the girl had never heard of the country.

"It is a country across the ocean. Across the water. It is very warm there too."

"Like here?"

"A little, yes."

"Then I will show my mother and my father your way with the injera when we return. Now it is my turn to rest. You must sleep."

Kari woke suddenly. Her feet had managed to work their way out of shade. They were hot in the sun beating down. She looked up and squinted.

Bilan had taken down the shelter. "It is time. We must go."

Kari stretched. Her legs ached.

"I rubbed my mother's special oils on your feet while you were sleeping."

"You did? I didn't feel a thing."

"I did not want to wake you. You needed the rest. Your feet will be better now."

Kari regarded the girl in a new light. "Thank you for doing that. I thought you had forgotten.

The girl stood up from her squat. Kari used her walking staff to help her stand. Her legs were aching more than she wanted to admit. "You will get accustomed. Let us go. I will walk slow to let you wake up."

Sometimes they walked side by side. Sometimes Kari walked behind.

Bilan still slowed to check on her progress. Kari appeared content with her methods, whatever method a woman from Scandinavia might have. "You are getting much better. When we get to the village, you will rest. It will be much easier for you when we walk back."

Kari wasn't so sure. She said nothing.

"There is one thing."

There was always one thing. One more thing. Kari couldn't bring herself to look at the girl.

"You must breathe through your nose. Much water leaves your mouth."

Why didn't she know that? Exasperated by her

ignorance of all things desert related, the crest of yet another dune appeared. Kari wasn't looking forward to climbing the monstrosity. The sand would be loose, and her feet would sink. She wondered if she should tell Bilan about snow and explain how deep one could sink into it.

"The village is beyond that dune. We already passed the marker my father showed me on the cloth."

They crested the dune. The rest of the trip would be all downhill. She was happy to see the other side—until she saw the trucks parked as though waiting for them.

"They are the ones who came to your father's encampment."

Bilan nodded.

Kari whispered, "Do not let them know I can understand their language."

Bilan didn't have time to answer. A gruff voice ordered them into one of the trucks. "We are taking you to the village."

But they didn't. The trucks got as far as the edge of the village and then turned away. They took them due south for what seemed like three or four miles. They halted at an encampment in the shelter of a rock overhang. At least half a dozen more trucks were parked beneath it.

"We should count the number of men, Bilan. And any weapons they might have."

The girl nodded. She had already done so. It

was not for nothing she was a clan leader's daughter. "I think our journey has come to an end, Kari. We must be very careful that we do not anger these men."

24

Iwas on base and about to turn to line up for final. I looked out over the camp and spotted a crowd gathered by the comms tent. I didn't think anything of it. I had already noticed the Porter wasn't parked on the strip. No doubt Mike was out keeping an eye on Kari and Bilan. He had to be staying in touch.

I taxied the 3 into its parking spot. Sammy commented about cheating death again. I was content to be home.

Sammy glanced at me.

"I'll get some of the guys to unload. For now, we'll keep them separate from the rest of the goods in the warehouse."

"Sounds good, Sammy. It's going to take a while."

The crowd was still in front of the comms tent. Unsure whether that was good or bad, I climbed out the cargo door and double-timed it. I didn't need to go the whole distance before I knew what was happening. I made my way past the collection of bodies to the radio. My heart pounded in my chest. The radio was manned by Jofre, one of our grizzled mercs. He brooked no shit, on the job or on R&R. He was armed to the teeth, ready for dispatch.

"What the hell is going on, Jofre?"

Jofre Belmont was one of our best, a reliable Catalan with more experience than Mike or I would ever have in both our lifetimes. I pulled back the tent flap. Two of our vehicles were parked at the side, out of sight. That's why I hadn't noticed them. Armed mercs milled about. Gazes shifted in my direction and the hushed conversations halted. I turned to Jofre.

He didn't avoid my glare. "You know Kari and Bilan headed off in the Land Cruiser to do their reconnaissance. Mike has been out doing high-altitude recon in the Porter since late yesterday. He saw the truck. It was stopped at the edge of a dune. Bilan must have known they couldn't make it over a fresh dune. The sand would be too soft."

"Smart desert girl, I'd say."

"I would say too. Two sets of tracks led up to the top of the dune and down the other side. They made quite a long distance to where someone was waiting for them. Their tracks disappeared. They became mixed in with a bunch more. At least four or five, as far as I could tell."

So Jofre had been on board the recon flight.

That was good. He knew what he would be looking at—or looking for."

"Did you have the glasses?"

The man almost growled at me. "I did. I saw with my own eyes." Obviously he thought I didn't trust his judgment.

"I believe you, Jofre. What do you think we should do?"

Grizzled veteran that he was, he didn't hesitate. "Mike has been up running a—how do you call it? Ah, a racecourse. He keeps high. I put a crew of good men in with him with the glasses. They are armed and ready to strike. The machine-gun is installed. I have placed a good man on that too."

What was I doing here? The guys had it well in hand. They were doing exactly what I would do.

"One thing, though, Harry. There was a huge sandstorm. It missed us. I think the women took refuge in a wadi to wait it out. That is why the dunes grew larger all of a sudden."

Bilan was an experienced desert dweller who could take care of herself. Her father wouldn't have permitted her to go otherwise. I felt confident she could look after Kari. Perhaps the hand-drawn map wasn't so accurate after all. The landmarks would have changed with the shifting sand.

There was nothing more to be done until Mike and his crew returned. "I'll take over the radios, Jofre. Take a break with your crew. If I need you—"

"No, Harry. No breaks. Kari stood by us on the radio when we needed her. We will stand by her."

"In that case, would you mind helping the guys unload the 3 before it sinks up to its wings in the sand? Sammy and I brought in quite a load. Have the guys refuel her too."

"I understand. We need to keep busy, is all. It will be done."

Jofre stood and called to one of his men. I didn't understand Catalan, but I knew from his tone and the response he got that the job was going to get done. I heard and understood Kari's name twice. That's all it took for Team Number Two to double-time it to the DC-3. They took their weapons with them. Everyone was prepared for anything.

That's what I like about these guys. When they say they're going to do something, they do it. No questions asked. Experience played into it too. Mike and I had been working with them for a long time. We all knew how we worked together. No one was afraid to make changes if or when they were requested.

That was the name of this game. Experience. A can-do attitude. A regular paycheck at the end of every month. A flight out for the occasional R&R. Simple. Efficient. Effective.

I made for the cook shack. I wanted to request early meals for the crew. Sandwiches and drinks to go if we had to land out there and stand by. The cook and his crew wouldn't be a problem. They were accustomed to our dealings too. When it had all been arranged, I still had one major problem.

Kari and Bilan were missing.

25

Kari couldn't get near the trucks. Each time she made an attempt, she was warned and threatened with a raised fist. It appeared to be for effect only. The threatened blow never landed, and she thought it odd that these men would not harm her or Bilan. What was keeping them from doing so?

She looked over the trucks as best she could from a distance. It appeared only three or four were in working order. The remainder were on stands or had flat tires. Junkers. Some even had rust. Perhaps they had a previous life in a seaside town or city.

What troubled her most was the two trucks with the machine-guns mounted on the bed. She had seen only one like it before. Harry wouldn't know about the second one, either.

Speaking of the devil. Where was Harry when she needed him?

Kari's thoughts were interrupted by loud voices. Bilan and a man were arguing. Something about a pouch. Then she remembered. It was the leather pouch Bilan carried around her neck. The signal mirror. Mike had given it to her. The girl was so proud, knowing she could signal Mike in the plane.

The voices grew louder. Questioning. Demanding.

"What is that for?"

Bilan's voice was just as loud. Shrill in her response. "It is not for men. It is for female things."

Would it work?

"Very well. You may keep it for now."

Kari sighed with relief. Bilan was a lot smarter than she gave her credit for. That didn't surprise her. Had she not taken them both across the desert sand in their truck and then by walking? She must remember not to underestimate the girl.

They were in a mess, though. The sandstorm had turned their trip into a disaster. No one back at camp would know where they were. Thank goodness Bilan knew the desert. But what would the men do with them? Would they keep them together? There were no other women in their camp from what she could tell. Was that good, or was it bad?

Two men approached and gestured for them to follow them to a tent. They were unceremoniously shoved inside. The floor was bare. Sand. Not like their camp in the slightest. Probably not like Diric's, either. Whatever this crew was up to, it wasn't setting up a camp intended for a long stay.

They sat on the floor, side by side, whispering. Bilan whispered first.

"These men are not nomads. Their camp is very poor. They will have little food. What they have has been taken from others."

So the girl noticed that too. Why am I surprised? "I saw it, also, Bilan. Their arms are old as well. Only two AK-47s. The rest are bolt action rifles."

But the two trucks with the machine-guns—Bilan didn't need to know her concerns about those.

"I do not understand such things."

"Trust me. Harry will be happy to know these things if we get to talk to him."

"I do not think that will happen so soon. At least it is cooler in here. You can rest your feet again."

They giggled like two schoolgirls. Kari wondered if Bilan would know what that meant. "Have you been to school, Bilan?

The girl hesitated. "Yes. I can read and write in Swahili and Somali. I am not very good."

"Did you like school?"

"Oh yes. Very much. I made many friends. We all went our ways when the caravans gathered. We had to help our families prepare for the trip we would all take to our clan grounds."

That was interesting. She thought back to her own schooling and learning about deserts and nomads and camels, and how they were called ships of the desert. She knew first-hand about it now.

"Do you think you will go back to school?"

"Yes. I will go back. My father and my mother insist that I do. My reading and my writing will get better the more that I study. My father is very proud of my abilities. My mother too. When she was young she did not have the opportunity. She prods my father. She wants me to have all the chances."

"I'm so glad to hear that. I think you will do very well. I am glad to hear your father and mother push you to go to school."

Perhaps the girl would be all right after all. There would be opportunities in the larger centers for a woman who could make friends, who knew how to deal with people. "It was the same for me in my country." But was it? Not a chance in hell, but the girl wouldn't know that. "My parents insisted that I go to school when I didn't want to. I was scolded all the time for missing my classes."

Bilan's ears perked up. "But why would you miss classes on purpose? Did you not want to be there?"

Kari knew the girl wouldn't understand the ways of western teenagers. Never mind Scandinavian teenagers. "I know better now. You know better. It did not take you as long as it took me to know better. That makes you smarter too."

Bilan blushed, uncomfortable with the praise.

"Your abilities and your experience got me through the desert sandstorm, Bilan. That is not a small thing. Without you, I would still be looking for—"

A captor raised the tent flap. They squinted against the light behind the man. A gruff voice assaulted them.

"Both of you will come with me. Now."

26

Mike knew the drill. He had the best squad on board the Porter, except for Jofre. The men were armed to the teeth with AKs and grenade guns. The .50 caliber machine-gun was installed and ready to go to work at a moment's notice. Before takeoff, Jofre made sure they had extra belts in cans. He had made sure it was test-fired too. There was no sense taking an inoperative weapon into battle.

He knew Jofre wanted to be on board. The man liked to be in on the action when he could. He was a team player who took care of his men. "This time I will stay back for Harry when he arrives, Mike."

The hard look on Jofre's face said everything. He wouldn't be trifled with if he got a chance at the men who had kidnapped Kari.

If she was kidnapped. They had little information to go on. Their Rover had been located from the air. It was obvious the women had made a tactical decision to proceed on foot, judging by the pair of footprints leading over the crest of the dune. Their feet had sunk deep into the fresh, loose sand. No vehicle could have crossed that dune.

He admired their dedication. He probably would have reversed course and returned to camp. He wouldn't have faulted Kari and Bilan for doing that. But they hadn't.

Mike put a call into base camp to learn that Harry and Sammy had returned in the DC-3. Soon there would be two airplanes in the sky. Two teams of men. He flipped on the intercom. "Any sign?"

The grizzled merc on station at the machine-gun hanging off the side of the Porter replied. "Nothing yet. I think we should shift the racetrack farther south."

Mike didn't even pause to think about it. "Not a bad idea, Iván. Consider it done."

He checked the fuel gauge. Tapped it. Shifted his gaze to look over the rest of the gauges. All were in the green. He titled the control wheel and fed in a little rudder. A wing dipped slightly. He locked in the turn. He wanted it to take forever. There was no purpose to alerting anyone on the ground with a flash of sunlight reflected by wing or window.

He pulled back the column and leveled the Porter. Checked the gauges one more time. They were good. "We're on station, Iván. Let me know."

"Si."

There was nothing. Hour after hour of nothing. How far could the women have gotten on foot? Darkness was approaching. That wasn't a problem. He could fly the Porter into daylight tomorrow morning if necessary. But he had nothing to show for the daylight he had burned. He stabbed at the intercom button, frustrated at the lack of a sighting. "Dammit Iván. I was sure we would have something by now."

"Perhaps it is for the best, Mike. Harry is back. Tomorrow we will have two planes."

Iván's tone told him he was just as frustrated. Iván had been with him when Kari was forced to man the radio when they needed help. She had got Harry in the air to bring reinforcements and get them all the hell out of the spot they had found themselves in.

Mike's voice came through the intercom again. "Tomorrow is a new day. We'll plan a fresh course of action with Harry's group when we get back."

Harry would be just as dedicated to finding Kari and Bilan. Already he could see the man kicking up sand in frustration with fading daylight. Night was fast arriving. No more than ten minutes and it would be pitch black but for the stars. He lined up on final in the purple light and touched down as night descended. He taxied opposite the DC-3 and shut down.

He was pleased to see the ground crew hovering

over the 3. It meant it would be ready to go first thing. He wasn't pleased to see Harry barreling toward him. "Did you see anything?"

Iván and his crew finished unloading the Porter.

Iván approached just as Harry got to Mike. "I think I might have spotted something, Mike. A wadi with a rock overhang. Erosion, most likely. It could be used as a campsite. Anyone beneath it would be invisible unless we were at the right angle."

Harry looked from Iván to Mike. The expression on his face wasn't good. "When did this happen? Why didn't you call it in? What the hell is wrong with you?"

Before Mike could answer, Iván spoke. "It was too close to dark, Harry. We had just extended our racetrack farther south and west. I caught a glimpse too. I had to be sure. *We* had to be sure. On the second pass I confirmed it was an overhang. Beyond that, I couldn't see a darn thing. We would need to be even farther south to get a look under it."

"He's right, Harry. It was getting close to dark. Even if we confirmed, we couldn't do anything about it. Tomorrow—"

"Tomorrow is a new day. First light. I want us airborne at dawn. Airborne and ready to fight. Let's meet in the comms tent after we eat. You can brief us all, Mike. You too, Iván. All of us will be interested to hear what you have to say."

Harry liked to include everyone in the discussion. It didn't mean he was open to any and all options, but it made the men—their men—feel as though they were participating.

27

It was too cold to sleep. I tossed and turned and shivered in the sheets. I kicked at them until they slipped off the cot to the canvas floor. I looked across in the dim light at Kari's empty cot. Told myself I would find her tomorrow. And Bilan. They went off as a pair, and by God, they would return as a pair. What is it they say? *Inshallah.* That's it. God willing.

And if God isn't willing, I sure as hell am.

But where are they? Tomorrow I'll send Mike and his squad off in the Porter to talk to the headman in the village where the pair were headed. If they aren't there—

I'll have to send Ali with Mike too. He'll be needed to translate. I hope Mike's crew is well-behaved. If they aren't, or if they show the slightest bit of doubt—

Hell, they would probably shoot up the village at the slightest misinterpretation of the facts. And I don't have any facts. Neither does Mike.

Damn it to hell and back.

I got out of bed, dressed, and made my way to the cook shack. I pulled back the flap. Every man I had was there ahead of me. They were armed to the teeth in preparation for the morning's flights. I looked around again. "Where's Mike? I need to talk to him."

"He'll be back. He went for a shower to clear the fog."

I used the time to brief the men as best I could. What I didn't know made it difficult. I made certain to emphasize that under no circumstance should anyone shoot up the village where we thought Kari and Bilan might be. "We don't know where they are. Until we do—"

I left it hanging, not knowing if that would be good or bad.

I still hadn't told Mike about Bryn and Maria. He had a bit of a thing for the woman when we were in Nairobi. He might not be happy with the bad news. I headed for the showers and banged on the door. "We need to talk, Williams."

We always used last names when it came to something difficult to digest. And letting him know about Maria would be tough.

Mike exited the shower with a towel around his waist. "Dammit, Delaney. Can't a man get cleaned up without being disturbed? I need a shave too. What the hell is it now?"

He turned away and made for his tent and I

chased after him. There would be no sugar-coating it. "Maria is dead."

Mike stopped in mid-stride. He turned to face me.

"Bryn shot her when he found out she didn't have the gems."

"That son of a bitch. Did you get him?"

I shook my head. "He got away on foot. Sammy managed to lob a couple of AK-47 rounds into his vehicle in the parking lot, so—"

"Did Sammy shoot her by mistake?"

"No. It was Bryn. He took off on foot after he shot her. I radioed the tower for the police. He wouldn't have gotten far on foot."

"If he didn't take a bootleg taxi."

That was true. There was a never-ending lineup of them for most of the day and night when flights arrived. "I'm sorry, Mike. I know you liked her."

"C'est la vie, Harry." That was our catch-phrase for just about anything that went wrong. "And thanks for letting me know."

I didn't dare say *You're welcome*.

"Everyone is on edge waiting for first light. They're all in the cook tent."

"I know. I was there before I left for my shower. When you get it together I'm going to go over the plan for tomorrow."

I didn't let on that I'd talked with the men already. He'd find out at the morning meeting when we went over the situation.

"In that case, don't forget to tell your squad not to shoot up the village. We don't know if the women are there. We don't know where they are."

28

Mike and I showed up in the cook tent in the early morning dark at the same time. The men hadn't left. They were drinking coffee and commiserating. I let them know how much I appreciated their loyalty and dedication to returning Kari and Bilan to the fold.

"It's going to be a long day." I hauled out an old Michelin paper map of the region from my flight bag. It was as good as any. It had some trails marked, as well as main roads. "This is the best I could do for a chart. We're left to our own devices as far as a reliable map is concerned. Mike and Iván have some information you're going to be interested in."

I was pretty sure Iván had already told them about finding the ridge and the overhang at the last minute yesterday. I stopped.

Mike gave Iván the nod.

"We moved the, how do you say, racetrack orbit? We moved south late yesterday. It was close to dark. At the last minute I spotted an overhang above a deep wadi. I think we should investigate. Perhaps the sound of our engine will, how you say, vibrate? No. Echo. The engine might echo if we get too close. It will send an alarm."

Iván hesitated. There was murmuring and then it ceased.

"We need to look for a place to land that is not too far from what might be a camp site. We can quick march into the wadi and locate a camp, if it is there."

Iván stopped and nodded at Mike.

"I'll be flying the Porter. We're going to have a squad with a sniper." Mike waited for the voices to quiet. I was pretty sure this was a new one on the crew. We had two snipers that could hit a dime from 500 meters. What we didn't have was a stable platform from which they could do that. "That's why we're going to get airborne before first light. The early part of the morning has the quietest air. If you've ever been on board one of our flights at daylight when you were hung over, you know those are the ones you want."

We had all been there at one time or another. Laughter erupted. It eased the tension in the cook tent only a little.

I spoke again. "Mike in Platform One will be airborne and on station at that wadi. Snipers, be sure to take as many rounds as you think you'll need."

I looked over the gathered men. All were nodding. Then I glanced at Iván. "Sorry to steal your thunder, Iván. I need eyes on that location if you were right. You'll get your reward, though. Mike and the Porter are first on the ground if there is a camp and men at that location."

All eyes were on me. I had one more thing I wanted to bring up. "When I was visiting Diric's camp, there was a truck with a machine-gun mounted on the back. This is what it looks like."

I didn't have the photos developed yet. I had forgotten with all the turmoil in Nairobi. Instead, I handed out a rough drawing. The men passed it around.

"That is something new for all of us. I have plans to acquire one when we get to Djibouti, but we're not there yet. We'll have to make do with the jury-rigged mount in the Porter. That's why it's essential that Mike is overhead in the Porter in case we need his firepower."

There was silence in the room as the men contemplated news of the gun-mounted truck. I went on with our marching orders.

"The DC-3 is Platform Two. If the air is stable, we'll also be over that wadi with a squad and a sniper. Sammy has been working all night to get the intercom rigged so both door positions can transmit on the radio if needed. That will eliminate the back and forth we usually do."

There was more murmuring from the gathered

men.

"Don't worry. It's no different than talking on the intercom. You'll be talking on the radio so either Mike or I can fly the airplanes to where they're needed with a minimum of fuss. In other words, we'll be covering you off if you're taking fire. I don't know if we will have a strip of ground suitable to land the 3. If we do, we'll be offloading and airborne as quick as we can to get the sniper back in the air."

Silence reigned, finally.

"Of course, be careful not to hit Bilan or Kari. If you're in doubt, don't fire or you'll have me to deal with when this is over. It's a long trek to anywhere you'll need to be to get away Scott-free. Pack lots of water."

The nervous laughter told the tale. That would hold them for a while.

"Oh. One more thing. Bilan has a signal mirror. Kari has a flare gun and a small automatic pistol—if they haven't been taken away. I'm certain Bilan will use the mirror. Her eyesight and her young ears have been honed by being raised in the desert. The girl will probably see us before we see them."

I let that sink in before I continued. "I was going to get Ali into the village. I don't think that's necessary now that we have a possible sighting by Iván."

"Any questions?"

29

I allowed Mike to take the lead while I warmed the twin fourteen-cylinder radial engines on the DC-3. I had Sammy as my co-jo in the right seat. He liked to be included in these things, even if he wouldn't take up arms until it became absolutely necessary. He preferred to watch the action from afar. I couldn't blame him. Or fault him. Mike and I both depended on him to keep our airplanes airworthy and in flying condition. If anything happened to Sammy, it would be tits-up for the operation.

Wheels-up saw the sun barely peeking over the horizon when I set power for a fast climb high into the sky. I wanted to keep the noisy DC-3 radials from being heard on the ground.

Mike radioed to report circling the wadi overhang at altitude. He'd seen a faint flash of light from beneath the overhang.

"That has to be Bilan."

I agreed.

"It only lasted a millisecond, but at least we know the whereabouts of one of them."

I climbed higher in the 3 and looked out the window. I had Sammy doing the same. The mercs in the back were busy too. I was desperate to find a place to land. If I couldn't get to Bilan and Kari in time—

Iván, Mike's spotter, called in a possible landing site. Mike came back to confirm. He was in position to put his crew overtop of the camp sheltered beneath the overhang. "They'll have a bit of a march, but the guys tell me it's nothing they can't handle. I'll be going with them."

That was a relief. Now all I had to do was get the damned hulk of a 3 on the ground and get busy. Why had I allowed those women to undertake that deal in the first place? Neither one was up to the task. A twelve or thirteen-year-old girl? And Kari? She had no damned experience walking around a desert.

Jofre, in the back, called out a possible landing site. He included distance and landmarks. I banked, hard. It wasn't easy in the lumbering DC-3. The airframe shuddered.

Sammy called a warning. "Easy, Harry. We don't want to lose anyone."

If they weren't holding on in back before, they were now.

I radioed Mike to confirm landing and position. I advised him we had about a three-kilometer march.

He didn't sound concerned. "I've quick-marched with your guys. It was all I could do to keep up the pace. Think of the bar stories you'll have to tell once we get into Djibouti."

Once again, I banked and cut throttle to the engines to slow. If need be, I would be in a good position for a landing. I wasn't committed, but I could be in a hurry if the spot appeared promising.

I kept eyes out the window during the bank. Experience told me the short-strip landing would be bumpy and rough on the old airframe. I pushed the column forward and reduced engine power even more. Added in some flap. I called for the gear, and after a wait that seemed much too long, Sammy called two green.

I eased her down as low and slow as I could, floating over the rough ground. The mains kissed the sand and we were down, bumping and grinding like a peeler in a strip joint.

I chopped the engines before we stopped rolling on the sand. I didn't want to announce our arrival any more than necessary. I made sure the nose was aimed at the camp. It would be our takeoff beacon.

With no need for an engine cool-down, already Jofre and his crew were on the sand with packs and rifles slung over shoulders. Compasses came out, and the men took bearings to the target. I had barely gotten my seatbelt unfastened.

The men were prepared to march. Sammy was prepared to wait.

"I'll keep the radio on, Harry. If Mike gets airborne first—"

"Roger that. You know where we keep the water. There's a spare AK over the bulkhead with enough taped mags to last longer than you'll need them. There's another AK hanging over the cargo door."

Sammy knew all that. "Don't be concerned with me, Harry. Find the girls and bring them home."

It made me feel good to tell him, anyway. I took my pleasures where I could find them.

The last time I looked, Sammy was sitting with his legs dangling out the cargo door, a stack of magazines at his side.

30

Sammy's parting words haunted me. *Find them and bring them home.*

Jofre's command brought me out of my reverie. "March or die, bâtards!"

I was certain he said it in English for my benefit.

Find them and bring them home.

Easier said than done. The finding was the easy part, thanks to Bilan's mirror signal. Easy, that is, if both women were being held at the encampment beneath the wadi overhang. If they weren't—

Mike called in that he'd spotted a truck on-site with a machine-gun mounted to the bed. It had to be the one I investigated when it showed up at Diric's camp. If we were airborne over the camp, that truck would present problems. On the ground, it would take one properly aimed grenade to take it out.

Jofre held up a fist. We halted and crouched in the uneven desert terrain. The advantage of even slight depressions in the sand to keep us invisible would be behind us too soon. A pair of binoculars appeared in Jofre's hands. He scanned both sides of the wadi before gathering us in a circle.

"We have better cover on the opposite side. I do not think we can take the time to get there. We have two options. *Primer*, first, descend into the wadi and follow it to their encampment. *Dos*. Climb down right on top of them. But we will take heavy fire in that case."

Option two and the casualties we would take while hanging from a rope wasn't a sell in my book. Jofre agreed.

"In that case, Harry, we will continue to march."

He waved an arm. Our squad of mercs, Jofre and I were on-course to confront the bandits head-on. As we got closer, the men separated into a V that would envelope the campsite.

Overhead, the quiet whine of the Porter's PT-6 continued unabated. Mike had to see what we were up to. I caught his wings waggling. It had to be his signal that he saw us. Still, I wondered if Bilan had hit him with her signal mirror a second time.

The air went silent.

What was Mike up to? Had he throttled back to land? Where was he going to put it? While I was over the site, I had my hands full with the DC-3. I wasn't looking for a place to put a Porter, even if it had been engineered for just such a mission.

I didn't have to wait long to find out. The Porter

appeared over the horizon. Mike had the nose pointed at the ground. He was aiming right at us. And he was descending at speed.

"Holy shit, guys. Mike is—"

To a man, they kept up their advance. What Mike was doing was no concern of theirs. Their duty was to Kari and Bilan.

The Porter's engine died. machine-gun fire raked the area beneath the overhang. Metal clanked. Jofre's V-formation kept advancing. He had figured on the truck being a prime target for Mike's gunner in the Porter. His squad was arranged in order not to interfere.

Mike held off the Porter until the last minute, then advanced the throttle. The PT-6 began screaming. He pulled up. Whoever was on the gun did a hell of a job. A smoke cloud began to rise over the gun truck.

The Porter banked again as Mike climbed it out of the wadi. He turned and ducked beneath the horizon. He had to be positioning to return for a second strafing run.

"All right. Let's get going. We need to find those women before Mike runs out of targets."

I raised the binoculars. Men were approaching the encampment from the opposite direction.

"Iván is on point. Who the hell is on that gun in the back of the Porter? He's doing a hell of a job."

We encircled the camp to meet up with Iván's squad. One by one, kidnappers were being dispatched. Still, there were no women. Where were they?

The sand moved in front of me. I readied an AK. Jofre held up a fist. I didn't relax. The sand settled. A face appeared. Bilan grinned.

"Jambo. We knew you would come. I will take you to Kari."

She didn't have to. Another pile of sand shifted only ten feet away and Kari pushed herself up and remained close to the ground.

"Hello, boys. What took you so long?"

Her boys didn't care. They high-fived her and lifted both women onto their shoulders.

Kari grinned. "Harry, let's get this show on the road. Who's back in camp minding the comms?"

That did it for the men. They laughed so hard they almost dropped her. The return march to the DC-3 was a lot quicker now that we had the women safe and sound.

Two mercs remained behind for cleanup. Gunshots echoed throughout the wadi.

No one asked any questions.

31

It didn't take the cleanup crew long to catch up. Overhead, Mike flew cover on our return march to the DC-3. The men were grateful for the air cover and the lookout. It might not have been necessary, but this was the desert. Warfare in such a place is treacherous.

Idling engines on the DC-3 greeted us. It was nice to know Sammy had been paying attention. I made my way to the cockpit while he helped the women and the still-outfitted mercs into the back of the 3.

I received a quick call on the headset to alert me that everyone was settled in. I was already applying full power when Sammy made it forward to join me. "It went pretty good by the look of everyone in back."

I nodded agreement. "We need to add one of those trucks to our inventory as soon as we can. Do you think Djibouti might come through for you in that department?"

"Truck? What are you talking about? We have trucks."

"I mean a gun truck. A machine-gun-mounted truck. One with a better gun than that piece of junk we removed from the back of this thing so we could close the cargo door."

I could see Sammy's wheels turning. He was thinking about it. I didn't bring it up it again.

Mike took up a position off our starboard wing and chased us home. It was uneventful but for one of our passengers.

Kari brought Bilan up to the cockpit to show her what was going on.

The girl looked from me to Sammy and back at Kari. "It does not look like they do very much, Kari."

Kari translated. Sammy looked across at me and grinned. I grinned right back. Bilan was right. Now that the job was done, it didn't look as though we did much up front in the office, as Mike and I called the cockpit.

Sammy got up and turned over the right seat to Bilan. He raised the seat and belted her in before pointing out the window at the Porter and Mike off to starboard. I alerted Mike, and he waggled his wings for the girl. I was pretty sure he could see the huge grin on her face as she looked out the window, waving frantically the whole time.

I alerted her we would be landing, and she watched, transfixed, as I set flaps and lowered the gear. It bumped into place, and I pointed as the two lights turned green. "That means our landing gear is down and locked." I knew she wouldn't understand what I was saying, but it made me feel good to point it out.

I was set up for a straight in approach. I pulled back the throttles. When the wheels kissed the sand, I taxied and killed the engines. Bilan was still grinning when I unbelted her and led her back to the cargo door.

Kari greeted her. "Harry makes it look as easy as making injera, right, Bilan? Mike does too."

Bilan said her thanks to the men and to Mike while Kari translated. The hardened mercs smiled and grinned and kicked at the sand, unsure of what to say to the girl. They mumbled and shuffled their feet and finally wandered off to the cook tent.

Kari made arrangements to return Bilan to her family in the camp's second Land Rover. The two drove off in a cloud of sand and dust, no doubt with a nervous father and mother anxiously waiting.

Kari looked across at the girl beside her. "Your father is going to be glad you are back home, Bilan."

"I too will be glad. I think our adventure is once in a lifetime, do you not?"

"You are right about that. Has any of it sunk in yet, or are you still thinking about what happened?"

"Oh no. I still want to be a teacher."

"Well, you will be a good one if the things you have taught me are any example. I will never forget the time we spent together. I won't forget the things you taught me about the desert, either, Bilan. You are a good person to teach such things."

Bilan blushed and said nothing. Kari brought the Land Cruiser to a halt beside Diric's tent. His wife rushed outside. A huge smile graced her face when she saw Bilan step out of the truck. "I am home safe, mother. Kari made certain."

"Praise be, daughter."

Diric joined his wife.

"Your daughter is an excellent teacher. She taught me many things about the desert that I could have never learned on my own. I will never forget her lessons."

Bilan blushed again. Her father placed a hand on his daughter's shoulder. "She teaches our young ones. I think she does a good job. She is careful not to go overboard with her teachings, although I think she would like to. Wouldn't you, daughter?"

"Yes, father, but I know I must obey too."

Kari nodded her understanding. "Well, I hope she will have a school house of her very own one day. She deserves it, as do her pupils."

"We hope so, don't we, daughter? We will see."

There was nothing more to be said. Kari got back into the Land Rover and started it.

Bilan leaned in to hug her.

Kari hugged her back. "I will make injera for Harry and Mike tomorrow, Bilan."

It was her mother's turn to blush as she turned to her daughter. "She taught you that?

"Yes. She told me all about it. I'm sure I will need some help for my first batch. We have kitchen helpers. I will ask. I will use Bilan's list of ingredients as she told them to me."

Kari put the Land Rover in gear and turned to wave before heading back to camp. Exhausted by the adventure, she could barely keep her eyes open by the time she pulled up to Harry's tent.

There was no reprieve. The entire camp of mercs, joined by Harry and Mike, greeted her. They hauled her off to the cook tent for an impromptu party.

It was midnight when Harry carried her to the tent.

32

Kari **couldn't sleep** in the night's unusually cold air. She shivered, even with an extra blanket she took from Harry's empty cot. She sat up, got out of bed, dressed and went outside. The beginning of a desert moon shone down on the camp, barely illuminating it.

Preparation for the camp move had already begun. Her drinking partners from the night's festivities, including Harry and Mike, were busy knocking down tents and packing boxes.

Trucks were being loaded. The cook tent was gone. So were most of the personnel tents. A bivouac arrangement had replaced them. It was strange she hadn't noticed the beehive of activity when she first got back. *Probably adrenalin*, she thought.

Kari sighed, went back inside, and began packing her duffel. *No rest for the weary* crossed her mind more than once. When she finished, she approached Harry.

"We're moving already? I thought—"

"We're moving north, the sooner, the better for all of us. The trucks will haul everything. I've paid off the local help. We'll find replacements when we land in our new region."

"When we land?"

"Yeah. We're headed to Djibouti for an R&R. The lot of us need something to take the edge off. Say, you look hot in that getup. Too bad we don't have a tent."

"Is that what you need to take the edge off, Mr. Delaney?"

"Well, it wouldn't hurt—"

"In that case, it's too-bad-so-sad we don't have that tent. Let's get packed."

"Already done. That's why we have all this help. Go wash up. It'll be the last chance until we make Djibouti. Then join me and Mike and Sammy and the guys. We're making plans."

Kari wandered off, and Harry's gaze followed her. Mike joined Harry as the pair surveyed what little remained of camp.

"I think she's the one, Mike."

Mike slapped his friend on the back. "It's about time, you old dog. New tricks, huh?"

"Well—"

"Never mind the *Well*. Get on with it before you get so old it's only a fond memory."

Harry gestured toward what remained of their campsite. "Easy for you to say."

"I just happen to have a life I enjoy."

A tent whooshed and collapsed, sending up a cloud of dust.

Mike grinned. "A wife would complicate things and put an end to all of this."

Harry waved an arm over what was left of their camp. "Yeah. I see what you mean. It's a wonder, isn't it?"

Mike didn't let up. "So then, you're going to run off like you always do? That's not gonna be easy, considering she's right here in camp with us. Didn't I overhear that you'll be taking her to Djibouti with the rest of the miscreants?"

"I can't very well leave her here, can I? And don't bug me. I'm thinking."

33

The DC-3's twin engines settled into a comfortable purr as Mike manually adjusted RPM to bring them into sync. He did it by ear. Satisfied, he nodded. They were at altitude. Cool air flooded the cabin. It was soon replaced by desert heat when Harry took command and set power for their descent.

Radio chatter overwhelmed their headsets. The men glanced warily at one another.

Mike spoke first.

"In Djibouti, desert meets the Gulf of Aden and the Red Sea, my friend. The city is full of drifters and outcasts from around the world. It's a safe hiding place for criminals. Gun runners and arms dealers too."

He looked at Mike. "Are you, old pot, calling this kettle black?"

The pair grinned at one another and Harry went back to the radio and chatter from the tower. "Did you hear what I just heard? I'd better let the men know. Take over, Mike." Harry left the right seat and made for the hold.

Not wanting to get shot out of the sky, Mike called the JIB tower and declared an emergency.

When Harry returned, the mercs busied themselves by donning battle dress and checking arms. Wooden crates creaked as the men pried them open for ammunition and grenades.

"The men aren't happy to learn our downtown hotel isn't available. But don't worry. Jofre and Iván came up with an alternative. It'll require a deuce-and-a-half."

Mike keyed the radio and made the request.

The response from the control tower was immediate. "You never heard that from us, Mike. You either, Harry."

"Guaranteed. The secret is safe between us and any other aircraft headed into or out of Djibouti on this frequency."

Mike went aft. He advised the men to keep the cargo door closed and to keep away from the windows.

"We've got a truck to take us downtown. Someone won't be happy we're taking it with us. On the plus side, think of the cab fare you'll be saving."

Laughter came from the grizzled veterans.

Iván stood to approach Mike. "Are you certain we should use a truck? We will be very noticeable that way, parading through the streets. Will it be covered? Perhaps—"

"You're right. Thanks for bringing that to my attention, Iván. Cars it will be. I can't make promises on what kind of cars."

Mike headed for the cockpit to apprise Harry of the change. He was in time to witness two green. "What am I doing here? You have everything under control."

"I need someone to talk me out of proposing."

Mike grinned and eased into the seat he had deserted only minutes before. "Then you hired the wrong man, buddy. The crew is a go for downtown. They want our hotel of choice back."

"Yeah, but only because they can walk back and forth to all the good bars, drunk or sober. Do you think the Place Menelik will be out of bounds?"

"Good bars? In Djibouti?'

Mike didn't appear to care that the Place might be off-limits. "Whatever works to keep them happy, Harry. Oh, and there's been a slight change. We're going in cars, not a truck. We'll be less conspicuous that way."

Harry wondered how that would work, but he knew not to ask. The men in back were the men with the solutions in that regard. They obviously weren't worried about being recognized for what they were while wearing desert camo and carrying AK-47s. Not to mention the BAR and the two sniper rifles.

He shrugged, and the DC-3 touched down.

"Hôtel, nous sommes arrivées."

Mike taxied to their usual out-of-sight spot behind and between two hangars. He used the torque to turn the 3 and aimed it between the buildings, pointing the nose in the direction of the runway. "Old habits die hard, mon ami. And if you need a quick getaway from Kari—"

Harry handed his friend a dirty look for the joke.

34

Harry cautioned the men against acquiring any of the deux chevaux in the tower crew's parking lot. He explained they would eventually have to fly out of Djibouti and back to camp. If the tower took a dislike to them, anything could happen. His men agreed, and three deux chevaux were requisitioned in the airport parking lot with nary a fuss but for relocated ignition wires.

"They look pretty good. Not a lot of rusty paint to be seen."

"Yeah, but that dull gray has got to go. Didn't Citroen have a color scheme?"

The three ancient vehicles groaned under the weight of the fully outfitted and armed mercs. Harry, Mike, and Kari climbed aboard, and suspensions sagged and groaned even more, unaccustomed as they were to the weight. Dashboard shifters were engaged, and convoy engines screamed complaints before slowly easing forward.

"I think we need to add a horse, gentlemen. See if you can flag down one of those donkeys.

"Your whining and complaining is louder than our engine, Harry."

Harry thought for a moment. "That's good, right?"

The men knew the route by heart. They made their way past a familiar landmark on the route to downtown. Mike gestured to the sand-colored, high-walled building with no windows and only a high double door.

"That emblem on the side of that place always intrigues me."

Jofre was quick to answer. "Why don't you bang on the gate and see what happens?"

"Non, Jofre, but merci for asking."

Jofre grinned, and Mike figured he knew more than he was letting on. In fact, he was pretty certain Jofre had spent time inside that very building.

Iván, in the lead, gestured to the curb. The trio of commandeered deux chevaux halted, a mere three blocks from the hotel. The mercs disentangled themselves from the folding roofs and tiny back seats and disembarked into the street. Magazines clicked and clicked again. Bolts slipped as rounds found chambers. Safeties rotated into place.

The men anxiously checked their timepieces. If a surprise attack was worth anything, this was going to be the one.

"All right. If you know anything, you know what's going on. We might get lucky. Where's Kari?"

She appeared with .45 strapped to her hip.

Harry noticed it and frowned. "Who gave you that?"

"Jofre. He taught me how to use it too. I can break it down in the dark."

I looked up at the man. He had a huge grin. "She is a valued part of the team now, Harry."

"Jofre, we need to talk later."

"Bien sûr, Harry. Of course."

The men checked each other's setups in silence. Shoulders were slapped. They were good to go.

Jofre called the command. "Alons-y. Let's go. March or die."

The men hauled ass and quick-marched through the streets toward the hotel. They slowed at a three-street intersection. Iván gave a hand signal. Without halting, Jofre's squad split from the group.

"If we can get to the hotel without arousing suspicion—"

Harry considered for a moment. "That's a big if, Iván."

Iván shrugged. "Everyone inside is going to be having themselves a little siesta, mon ami." He hesitated. "Qu'est-qe vous pensée? What do you think?

Silence. The men were more than ready. I was

pretty certain they had the same idea. They marched on. The two groups arrived at the hotel at the same time. Circled it. One squad went in the back. The second went in the front. Mike and I, together with Kari, remained at the front of the brick building.

In mere minutes, one of Jofre's men came out to tell us the main floor had been secured.

We met in the lobby. The mercs grabbed keys from behind the front desk, disabled the phones, and assured the panicked clerk he was safe. That they wouldn't be long. The shocked clerk nodded too fast and seemed happy to hear it before scooting out the door.

Men climbed stairs. Doors opened. Other men still rubbing sleep from their eyes were herded downstairs and into the lobby. Arms were collected to be stored later in basement closets.

"Just as we thought, Harry. Siesta. No need to fire a shot. We will post guards, but judging by the reaction of *les miserables*—"

Jofre gestured toward the prisoners. "I don't think we will have any problems. Mais—" Jofre appeared crestfallen. He gestured across the street to a small, off-white building. It looked the worse for wear. Windows were broken. Bullet holes scarred the block walls.

"C'est fermée."

The small building had become a favorite of the men during their visits to the city. Ice treats.

Cigarettes. Chocolate bars. Coca. It didn't matter whether they were hung over or just getting up.

Harry observed the shop through the hotel door. It was more than closed. It was obvious someone had used it as a fortress to rain down gunfire on the downtown sector. Judging by the bullet holes and the blown roof, the building had taken a lot of punishment, though it was still standing. A woman and a girl stood back, regarding the place.

"Those must be the owners. Kari—"

"Your wish is my command, general. We will have gelato by tomorrow."

Harry didn't doubt it for a minute. "Before you go, can you explain to our prisoners in their native tongues that it would be best for them to return to their families? I'm pretty sure they'll be welcomed with open arms when they find out they are safe and sound and can go back to their jobs, if they have any."

Harry approached Mike in the lobby. "Have you seen Kari?"

Mike shook his head. "I haven't seen hide nor hair of her since we secured the hotel. Did she sneak off to do some shopping?"

Mike threw Harry a dose of side-eye. "Yeah, that's a definite no. If she heard that, you'd be dead meat."

Mike gestured toward the hotel entrance. He couldn't suppress the grin. "She's across the street with the family that owns the gelato shop. She's helping them get it ready for opening."

Harry walked to the hotel door and peered past it. Already Kari was busy shoveling cement and mixing it in a trough. She leaned on her shovel and swiped at her forehead with a forearm. She looked good in the sweaty t-shirt and cargo pants. The .45 hanging off her hip at a rakish angle added to the mystery.

"Look at her, Harry. Those women and the

little girl get along like they were sisters."

Harry stood back to admire Kari. "I noticed that too. She was the same with Bilan and her mother. I'm going to ask her tonight, Mike."

Mike regarded his friend and played dumb. "Ask her what?"

"You know what. I'm going to ask her to marry me."

"That's good and all, but do you have a ring?"

Harry hadn't considered that. "Hell no. Do I need one?" He bettered his excuse. "Besides, I wouldn't know what size to get."

Mike grinned a shit-eater. "I'll go ask her for you." He faked a move toward the door.

Harry caught his arm and swung him around. "Fat chance, my friend. I'll figure something out."

The men returned to the lobby to confirm the hotel was secured. Everything appeared to be in order.

Sleepy revolutionaries had been dispensed with. They had shed no blood. It might not have satisfied his men, but he definitely was. The captured arms had been secured in downstairs closets, out of sight and out of mind. They had snipers on the roof. The front desk was properly occupied by surprised and satisfied hotel management. Everything was going to plan.

"You know, Harry, when it gets out that our men took the hotel without firing a shot, they'll never buy another round of drinks for as long as we're here. The story alone will be unbelievable."

"Never mind that. When word gets out that the gelato store is open again, Kari will be able to join them in the merry-making for sure."

A truck filled with troops screeched to a halt across the street in front of the gelato shop. Armed soldiers disembarked. Kari ignored them and continued mixing the cement. She only looked up to see the approaching captain.

"Bonjour, mademoiselle."

She halted. Dug the shovel into the cement mixer. The .45 in its canvas holster still hung off her right hip at a jaunty angle. Her hand moved to it and halted, resting on the closed flap. "Bonjour."

Alarmed soldiers readied their weapons. The captain waved a hand, signaling them to stand down.

"It is forbidden to own or possess arms in Djibouti, mademoiselle. Do you not know we have had an insurrection?"

Kari smiled sweetly at the man and his troops. "Mais bien sûr, Capitaine." She called to the little girl sweeping the gelato shop grounds and smiled at her. "Yasmiin. Gelato pour les soldats, s'il te plaît."

The girl smiled back. "Si, Kari. Bonjour, messieurs."

Kari brought two fingers to her lips to feign smoking. Yasmiin smiled and nodded and skipped into the shop. The girl returned with a tray of gelato and cigarettes. "Voulez-vous des cigarettes? Gitaines. Gauloises. Rothmans."

Kari turned to regard the girl. A broad smile greeted her. Kari nodded her approval and regarded the heavily armed soldiers. "N'oubliez-pas de payer la petite, mes amis. Don't forget to pay."

She patted the .45 hanging off her hip and headed for the hotel. She did an about-face and skipped past the men. The captain followed Kari to the hotel. Harry greeted him before he got to the front door.

Kari went upstairs as Harry addressed the captain.

"Bonjour, Capitaine. How may I be of service?

In the background, Mike rounded up the men and waved the desk clerk away. Weapons clattered behind the front desk.

"I was told you took the hotel without firing a shot. I came by to congratulate you and your men. I would like to inspect them, if I may."

"Of course. Give me a minute, please."

He hurried into the lobby. Jofre and Iván had been eavesdropping on the conversation. They formed up the men in two lines. Both men stood to attention at the end of his line. There was an empty space beside Jofre. Confused, Harry gestured to it.

Jofre called up the stairs.

"Karita. Downstairs, s'il vous plait. Vite!"

Kari rushed down the staircase. Her colorful

yellow and blue dress swirled behind. Jofre gestured to the space between him and his line of hardened mercenaries. She took up her place and stood at attention. The .45 remained at her hip. In her rush to answer Jofre's urgent call, she had strapped it on, not knowing what to expect.

Harry gestured for the captain to proceed into the lobby. He took up a position beside Mike and waited. The captain walked down the line of men. He hesitated in front of four. A brief, almost imperceptible nod passed between them, including Jofre and Iván. The captain saluted. Harry's men respectfully returned it.

"Well, Harry Delaney and Mike Williams. You and your crew have certainly done an admirable job. I don't think I have to mention that the first round of drinks will be on me *ce soire* when all of you make it to Place Menelik."

He strolled back to Kari.

"Mademoiselle, you have forgotten to store away your, umm, *votre sac à main*. Your purse."

He gestured toward her hip.

Kari blushed. She didn't like to be caught and scolded a second time about her sidearm. "Mais oui. I got called downstairs and dressed in a hurry. I was uncertain what the men might need. It will not happen again."

"Très bien. Very well then. Your dress is very pretty."

"Merci, monsier." She blushed a second time

and curtsied.

"Captain, I am giving free dance lessons tonight. You and your men are invited."

Renaud halted, considering. "I don't think my wife would approve."

"Well then, you will bring her, won't you?"

Capitaine nodded and proceeded to join his men outside. The truck started and drove off. Kari called to Yasmiin. "Did les soldats pay the bill, ma petite?"

"Oui, Kari. Le Capitaine a payé."

Several hours later, the captain returned without his men. "Harry, I have something for Mademoiselle Kari. I think she will like it."

Harry called up the stairs to Kari, and she joined him in the lobby. She nodded to Renaud. "What is it?"

"The captain has something for you."

"I noticed your handgun is quite large for your hand. I brought something you might enjoy a lot more." He held out the holstered semi-automatic wrapped in a web belt. "It is much lighter and more likely to fit better in your hand."

Kari clipped the belt closed around her waist. She withdrew the pistol. Eased back the slide to see there was no round chambered. Released the empty magazine. Hefted the pistol. "It is much lighter."

The captain nodded. "It will be so even when it is loaded. I have a spare magazine for you too. I noticed yours tucked into your, umm, brassiere." Renaud blushed, but he recovered quickly. "It takes 9mm ammunition. I have two boxes for you. There is one thing, though. I must show you the safety."

He held out his hand for the pistol, and she handed it to him.

"It is a MAC50 and it has—how do you say?—a bit of an oddity. It is quite easy to apply the safety while pulling back the slide to chamber a round. Such an error could get you killed." He demonstrated. "You must always carry the pistol with the safety on, no matter your battle condition. You will always flick the safety off with the thumb, even if a round has just been chambered."

He looked at Harry, who nodded his approval.

"You must always assume the safety is on and must be flicked off prior to firing. It will take a bit of practice to become accustomed. I think you will prefer it over the bigger and heavier .45 that you carry."

Kari handed off the package to Harry while she hugged Renaud. "Thank you very much for the gift. I expect to meet your wife tonight, Captain. Was it your personal weapon?"

"Yes. But I did not tell you that. My wife and I will see you all tonight."

36

The men ceased their grumbling, satisfied with the results of the inspection by le capitaine. They were certain he had been searching for the weapons they had hastily stashed behind the hotel desk. In he had found and taken them, the backup plan had been to retrieve the arms of the revolutionaries they had stored in the basement. Fortunately, they didn't need to act on it, thanks mostly to Kari.

They were still wary of their surroundings. They dispatched patrols around the hotel. A mercenary accompanied the desk clerk. The clerk knew the regulars, and they were allowed to check in.

Arms ended up strategically placed behind the desk in close range in case they were needed. A man each at the front and rear entrances to the hotel remained on guard. A sniper lounged on the roof, to be summoned by a call on the walkie-talkie.

Those without assignments crossed the street to the gelato store and the little girl and her mother.

The girl's happy smiles greeted them as she served up cold treats under the watchful eye of her mother. Cigarette sales added to the smiles. She told the men to thank Kari for her help.

Kari surveyed the men from the top of the staircase. Her dress billowed as the breeze floated up the stairs. Draped over one arm were some cloth items. She did a Marilyn Monroe and made a successful grab for the loose skirt. She called down to the men.

"We are all going dancing tonight. No excuses. Anyone who doesn't know how to dance will get free lessons. No boots. Avec chaussures seulement, mes amis. Shoes or sneakers. Pass it on to everyone." She hesitated. "Before I forget, I have a little something for each of you. If you don't like what you get, I won't be insulted if you trade."

She called the men to attention. When they had formed up in two grinning ranks, she stepped in front of each man as if inspecting him. She handed each a Hawaiian shirt. To a man, no one complained. Or traded.

After the impromptu ceremony, Harry announced that he and Mike would take the first shift. "The rest of you can decide who else will remain to guard our accommodations. I propose a shift change every three hours. But if anyone is a little late, no worries."

There were no complaints about the extended watch.

Harry opened and checked the timepiece he had carried across East Africa. It was a small pocket watch, in gold.

Kari grinned and provided a rejoinder to Harry and Mike. "Don't worry, you guys. I will try to convince your replacements to return early. Your dancing shoes will get a workout too. Alons-y, tout le monde. It is time, everyone."

She linked arms with two of the grinning men in their bright Hawaiian shirts. They marched in step to the Place Menelik, where bars and shops were only beginning to open.

Harry took out his watch a second time. It was just after 0200. The more things changed, the more they remained the same. And the way things were shaping up, it was going to be a very late night indeed.

Kari rolled over in bed and groaned. She kicked off the damp sheets and felt for Harry. Her hand slipped beneath a pillow and closed on a .45. She withdrew her hand and rolled upright, putting her feet on the floor.

She groaned again and called to Harry. "What time did we get back last night?"

He grinned as he handed her a glass of water. "Last night? Surely you jest." He found his pocket watch again and flipped it open. "Almost noon, my sweet. What would you like for lunch?"

He twisted the stem, winding the watch, and chuckled. He already knew she wouldn't be wanting lunch. "Perhaps a little petit déjeuner?" He flipped the watch closed.

Kari knew exactly what he meant, even in her hungover condition. "No little déjeuner for you, Mr. Harry, petit or otherwise. I'm going shopping. I need a new dress since everyone has seen me in this old rag." She gestured to the foot of the bed where she had discarded her dress. It lay in a wrinkled pile.

She had danced the feet off of Harry's men. There were no complaints. Even the capitaine had showed up with his wife. His promise of free drinks had come to fruition. It was only one of many reasons Kari was so hung over. He didn't doubt his men were in even worse condition. "In that case, you might want to wait a bit longer. Stores are just opening shutters at this hour."

"Then I have time for a shower." She gestured. "After you, my good man."

Hungover as he was, Harry stripped down in record time. The water was icy. He had forgotten to flip the circuit breaker on the water tank. He didn't mind. It made for some unusual goosebumps on his partner in crime. He skipped out of the shower and dressed to head down the street to a patisserie for brunch. He returned with warm croissants and cheese and tea.

Kari had showered and then put on the dress from the night before. "I swear, Harry. You are too good to me."

"You wouldn't have said that when you finished with those invoices you tallied after I set fire to them. Remember that?"

Kari smiled. Indeed, she did remember. "Well. Those were different times, were they not? There's plenty of sand under the bridge now." She washed down the last of the croissant with a swallow of tea. "Okay. I'm off in this old rag." She twirled in last night's dress for Harry. "I'll be back in time for siesta."

Harry only smiled. "Promises, promises."

He dispatched two of his crew to keep an eye on her. There was a revolution going on, after all.

37

Harry ended up in the lobby, still hung over from the night's festivities.

Mike presented him with a glass of hot tea.

"Did you get cinnamon and rock sugar?"

"Oui, monsieur."

Harry regarded his friend. "Cloves?

"Bien sûr. And I made sure yours has the dead fly. Just the way you like it."

Mike had been by his side on that escapade. In fact, Mike had been by his side on most, if not all of them.

"You would. I still remember the first time we met with that clan leader. Was it really all that long ago?" Harry reflected before going on. "Anyway, I stared at that fly in the glass as I brought it up. There was no way I could turn it down."

"Better you than me, old friend."

"Yeah, but I figured it was well sterilized in that boiling water. I was more concerned about dropping the hot glass and spilling it in my lap than

I was about the fly."

Mike raised his glass. "Old times."

Harry repeated the gesture. "Old times."

The explosion rattled windows in the hotel. Harry and Mike rushed into the street. A huge plume of smoke rose over the shopping district.

"Holy shit! Kari is out there somewhere! Two of the men are tailing her. I asked them to keep an eye on her."

"I'll grab one of the deux chevaux. Load some arms from the hotel and I'll pick you up here."

Harry and Mike, joined by the two men guarding the hotel, made for downtown. They dodged people and finally had to desert the Citroën on a side street blocked by debris. They armed up and proceeded on foot.

"Son of a bitch, Mike. That bomb was huge. What do you think it was?"

"No idea, but I hope there's not another one. We'll be toast."

Troops guarded the site of the explosion.

Harry eyeballed the crowd, searching for his men. He recognized the shirts and rushed to them. "Where's Kari? Is she with you?"

Jofre and Iván were beside themselves. "The plan was to meet her at the café. Merde. She went there ahead of us. We asked her to wait, but she wouldn't. If she had—"

Harry knew then.

"If she had only waited, Harry—"

Harry recognized the look on the faces of his two squad leaders. They blamed only themselves. "It's not your fault. I know what she's like. We'll find her. She's probably in a store somewhere. Let's spread out if we can get past the guards."

Harry forced his way through the confusion. Past bloodied people milling about. He climbed onto the raised patio, where he recognized Kari's dress from yesterday. He whistled and waved to Mike and his men. "Over here!"

He made his way to Kari's inert body and bent over her. She lay on the ground, with her head on an outstretched arm. It was as though she was asleep. There wasn't a mark on her that he could see. Even her shoes were on her feet. He picked her up in his arms and cradled her. "She almost made it out of the building. She had to be running away. Someone must have left a bag beneath a table and run off. Look." He pointed. "Over there. The hole in the floor."

Harry carried her out to the street. His men formed a protective cortège around Harry and the woman in his arms. Mike and Jofre and Iván cleared a hasty path through the crowded street. Rifle butts found their mark against bystanders who refused to move out of the way.

"She almost made it, Mike. She was out the door and on her way into the street. She almost made it."

Blood covered Harry's shoulder where Kari's

head rested. "Dammit to hell and back. Someone is going to pay. Or the whole damned city will pay."

The men made their way to the hotel, where Harry placed Kari on the front desk. "Get me a sheet. Fast, dammit!"

Yasmiin and her mother were silent observers to the goings-on from across the street.

"Mike—"

Mike returned with a sheet to cover the woman. He ordered the hotel closed. Staff paraded into the street. He closed and locked the doors behind them.

The men broke off to let their comrades know what had happened. In minutes, the battle-hardened soldiers surrounded Harry and Mike and their deceased friend.

"We have a job to do, Harry. None of us will rest until it is done."

Mike answered a knock on the hotel door. It was Yasmiin, there to offer her help if it was needed. "My mother will help too."

"Thank you, Yasmiin."

Mike said, "We need both of you to go out and listen for news about what happened at the restaurant downtown."

"Pas de problème, Harry. We will do it."

"Thank you. Someone will speak of their success with the bombing. We need to know who it is."

"I will come back. You can count on me to help

you learn who murdered my friend. I will come back."

Harry ordered one squad to guard the hotel. He took the remainder with him. Not a one discarded the shirts. The sight of a heavily armed convoy of men proceeding through town in beat-up deux chevaux caused tongues to wag. It must have been the wrong tongues.

Capitaine Renard arrived at the hotel with a contingent of his men. He had arrived at the blast site only slightly before Harry had. He recognized the shirts from the night before. Already he had confirmed the victim. He also knew the consequences of what had happened. He approached Mike.

"Is Harry here?"

"No. He has taken his men for lunch. They will be back later. I will tell him you came by."

"I am afraid you are going to have to accompany me."

Mike's men, on overhearing the conversation, surrounded him. He waved them off. "In that case, from what you have just witnessed, you'd better have a battalion to commit. You saw how my men treated Kari yesterday during inspection. They won't rest for a minute until they have their revenge. They won't care who they take it out on. Neither will I."

"Perhaps you are right. In that case, be sure your men remain in the hotel. I will see that we treat your comrade properly. I will leave a man here to message me." Renard knew he would have his hands full with Harry and Mike and their men. There would be no rest for any of them until they found the guilty party and lined them up against a wall. "When you find them, I do not want to know. Compris?"

When Renard and his men departed, Mike dispatched four of the second squad in pairs to make inquires at the local bars. "Fair warning, guys. If you go armed, you might encounter des petits problèmes, n'est-ce pas?"

The men grumbled before dumping handguns tucked into belts on the table in the lobby. Mike was pretty sure knives, brass knuckles and pistols in ankle holsters remained, but that was no concern. The men knew what they were doing. And he knew what they were capable of, even with the limited resources they kept on their bodies.

"Soyez prudent, okay? Be safe."

Harry turned the Citroën around and made for the hotel. There was no news in the bars they had stopped at. It was the same with the open cafés. "We've come to a dead end, men. We have to regroup."

The hotel was vacant. The remaining two Citroëns were gone. Harry's disappointment was palpable. His men had fanned out across the city without him in search of fact or rumor concerning who had set off the bomb.

Inside, he found Mike. "I'm done, Mike. Finished. I've had enough. I'm taking the DC-3 to Casablanca. You can come, or stay with the ragtag bunch of mercenaries. We hired them to do a job, but that job is done. I'll canvas them and see who wants to get the hell out of here with us."

"What about Kari?"

"She has no family. I'll get her cremated and scatter her ashes to the winds after we're airborne. Are you good with that?"

Mike nodded. "I'm good with that."

38

The men survived on tea and coffee and croissants and injera and whatever else Yasmiin and her mother could provide. Harry remembered how Kari had gotten along with the girl and her mother. He made sure they had an ample reward for their services. The duo turned out to be a fountain of information that they passed on in whispers to Harry and Mike, and to their men when they weren't there. Those secrets were part of the reason the men had no sleep.

Mike said, "If we don't get some results soon—"

Harry wasn't having it. "We'll sleep when we're dead, Mike. If you want to take the DC-3 and whoever wants to go with you and make for Casablanca, I'll see you there once we're done with whoever remains behind to clean up this mess."

"You know that's not what I meant. Yasmiin and her mother are goldmines of information. I'm hoping we'll solve this thing by tomorrow. We should be airborne—"

"I don't want to hear it. Tomorrow. The day after. Do we have anywhere else we need to be?"

Iván ran into the lobby. "I think we have a solution, Harry." Iván nodded to Mike, as though hoping Mike could control his friend.

"Are you certain?"

"Si. I think we have good information, thanks to Yasmiin and her mother."

"Then no one must know. It would be very dangerous for them if anyone found out they were helping us."

"I agree. We should be ready to depart the country at a moment's notice."

Mike stood up. The walkie-talkies he had convinced Harry to buy would finally be put to good use. "I'll get hold of Sammy and tell him to have the plane fueled and oiled and inspected. He'll have the engines warm for us at a moment's notice. He's going to want to know how much fuel to put on."

"Tell him it's Casablanca or bust. No freight. Men only."

An ancient, rusted-out deuce-and-a-half groaned to a halt in front of the hotel. Doors on rusty hinges screeched open. Armed men disembarked. One forced a groaning tailgate down. The rest began loading the weapons stashed in the hotel's storage.

Mike popped the hood and yanked out the oil dipstick. He began dripping oil onto the tailgate hinges. When he finished, he moved on to the doors. "Where the hell is that thing going to take you guys?"

"Mike, don't be asking questions the men don't want to hear. It's enough to know we're going to be getting our sweet revenge. Get on board or get out of the way."

Harry was obviously hurting. He had been walking around in a daze for hours. That he hadn't tumbled off the wagon and into the nearest bar was a concern.

"I should have gone with her, Mike. It's all my fault. Iván and Jofre—"

Mike stepped in front of Harry, temporarily halting his frantic pacing. "You know what Kari was like. She could outrun any of us. She was hell-bent on finding a dress. The two of us couldn't have blocked her way. Jofre and Iván were no match, and you know it."

"I know. I know. Still—"

"She knew the hazards. Remember how the three of us got up at the same time in the Stanley's café? She knew."

It was true. Harry knew it.

"She made it as far as the door, Harry. She knew what was going down. She was trying to get away."

Harry sighed. His shoulders slumped. "Maybe I am going overboard or—"

"No. You're not. But it's going to be a while until things around here are back to normal—whatever that is."

Harry knew not to cross Mike. Or the men. All of them had taken a liking to Kari, and having their revenge play out would be good for morale. Neither he nor Mike made mention of Casablanca. They would wait until the job was done.

39

It nearly broke Sammy's heart when he learned what happened to Kari.

Last night—*dance night*, she called it—had been an enormous success. She had gone out and bought Hawaiian shirts for all *her* men, as she called them. Where she had found the shirts, only she knew. She had told them she wouldn't dance with a single one until they put on the shirt. The woman had tamed the rag-tag team of dangerous mercenaries, to be sure.

There was no doubt Harry and the crew would be out for revenge any way they could find it. He was certain they were fanning out across the city in search of informants. Perhaps Yasmiin and her family might even be capable of helping. They had taken a liking to Kari too.

Sammy shook his head to clear his thoughts. It was time to prepare the DC-3 for departure. If history was anything to go by, that notice could come at any time. He wanted to be ready.

He busied himself topping the plane's fuel, oil and hydraulic fluid levels. He borrowed a forklift and loaded a drum of hydraulic fluid, just in case. It took some effort, but he rolled it forward on his own and then blocked it with a piece of wood. He'd get the men to help stand it upright. In the meantime, he tightened the bungs to prevent leakage. He searched for and located the hand pump for the thick fluid where it should be in the spares chest.

Experience told him Casablanca would require at least one stop to re-fuel. He climbed the steps to the tower, looking for a former acquaintance. Luckily, the man was working, and that's when he learned they would need three refueling stops. The 3,000 nautical mile distance was just out of range of two stops—and that was if they encountered no wind or weather to slow them down.

Next, he went to check the teletype looking for en route weather problems. That's when he learned about a Sahara windstorm that was forecast to blow up within the next three days. To put it mildly, that wasn't good.

Sammy turned on the walkie-talkie and adjusted the squelch. He made a call to both men, hoping to make contact for an update. There was no response.

He walked down to the empty chart room and pocketed 1:500,000 aviation charts to get them to Casablanca and no farther. He carried them to the plane, unfolded them, and began looking for the obvious refueling stops along the way. If he could find three or four reliable airports—

That was the problem. Reliability. In these troubled times, there was little of it.

Something that had been bothering him clicked. Sammy grabbed a Phillips screwdriver and walked aft to the inspection plate on the DC-3's floor. He undid the screws and lifted the plate. There it was. Harry must have put it back. He felt the bag and tried to count through the thick canvas. There were too many. Grinning, he replaced it and screwed down the plate. He brushed the dust and sand into the crevices. A quick glance would tell anyone looking that it had never been opened—if they even knew about it.

He tried calling the guys again. Still nothing, and that worried him.

Sammy headed back to the tower. There was no substitute for the scuttlebutt those guys could pass on regarding friendly airports.

40

Yasmiin hurried across the street to the hotel in search of Harry and Mike. She didn't find them. Les mercenaires greeted her, and she began telling them about what she had discovered and what she had seen. She stuttered at first, unsure of how the men would treat her. She needn't have worried. One giant of a man picked her up and placed her on the hotel desk. The others gathered around.

"Do you have information for us about some people we need to do business with?"

She hesitated. "Oui."

Jofre said, "T'inquiète pas, ma petite. We are here for you. Harry and Mike will be back shortly." He waved a hand, and the men disappeared up the stairs, still wearing the Hawaiian shirts. In minutes, they had packs shouldered and weapons armed and ready to go.

"Très bien, ma petite. Nous sommes prêts. We are ready."

The girl grinned a silly grin at the colorful shirts. "Do you have new battle dress? You do not resemble any troops I have seen."

"We do this for Kari. Only for Kari."

Harry and Mike came through the hotel door, halted, and took in the circus.

Harry said, "What's going on?" He spotted Yasmiin sitting on the front desk. "Why are you— never mind. You have news of Kari?"

Yasmiin nodded.

The sight of the men still in the colorful shirts revealed their soft spot for their radio operator and dance instructor. Harry was taken completely aback at this display of affection for Kari by the battle-hardened crew.

Jofre repeated what the girl had told him.

"And she's willing to lead us to them? I'm not certain that's the safest—"

"We will consult with her mother first before we put anyone in danger." Jofre turned to the girl. "Come, Yasmiin. I hope you are a fast talker."

It turned out she was. Yasmiin's mother and the girl climbed into the passenger seat of the beat-up troop carrier. Directions came in French to Harry. There was much excitement generated when he sometimes mixed up à droite et à gauche for right and left and had to backtrack.

Eventually, the pair told Harry to halt on a side street in a warehouse area on the outskirts of the city. It was an older part. Houses were few and far between, instead replaced by warehouses and other smaller buildings.

"Follow me."

Yasmiin and her mother directed the men behind piles of stacked wood before gesturing to the huge warehouse. "That is the place."

Harry nodded. "Very well, Yasmiin. We will take care of it from here. You must return home with your mother. You cannot be associated with us in any way. It is not safe. When we are gone from here, I need to be sure you and your family will be safe."

His fractured French got through to her with help from Jofre's translation.

She hugged Harry and Mike and then Jofre before moving off. Harry saw the wheels turning. There was no way she or her mother were going to miss out on the certain retribution.

There was nothing more he could do to change their minds. "I know you are grateful for Kari's help with your store but—"

Yasmiin's mother waved him off, and he gave up.

The men placed the building under observation. They took turns on watch while others slept or paced or cursed.

It took a day and a night. The final count came in at 15 or 20 wandering in and out. Some stayed. Some came and went. The mercs didn't care. They would take care of them all, given enough time.

Harry's team had learned the lesson well from the hotel takeover. They hit the warehouse during siesta. There were no guards. No booby traps. No women or children on lookout. There was, however, one child present. Yasmiin had refused to return home. They didn't spot her observing their actions.

Yasmiin kept a cold eye on the men in their happy shirts, as she called them. She prayed they would be successful in avenging her friend's death.

"Inshallah," she added. God willing.

She remained at her position, crouched behind stacks of wood. She knew it would be a long wait, but it was all she could do. She wanted to see for herself that Kari's killers would face justice. She took some of the injera from her pack. She had made Kari's recipe for the sauce. The taste was different now, but still very good. She licked her lips.

The wait grew longer. Yasmiin stretched and yawned and rubbed her eyes. She sat up and peered past the edge of rock and bricks and stacks of wood. She had slept. She didn't know for how long. A man moved beside her. The motion startled her until she recognized the shirt. It was Jofre, the man who had lifted her onto to the desk in the hotel.

"You should not be here, ma petite. It is not safe."

The huge blast rocked Yasmiin's lookout spot. Jofre threw himself on top of her.

Bricks shook and rattled. Woodpiles tipped over. She closed her eyes and covered her face against the heat and light. When she finally opened them again, she found herself looking up at a small patch of blue sky. A cloud of black smoke and dust obscured the remainder. It slowly drifted away toward the city in the slight breeze.

She smiled as she clawed her way from beneath the man. She forced herself to crawl to the wall that had protected her. The building was no more. It wasn't even a pile of rubble. It had disappeared completely, as though God had taken it away. The outbuildings were gone too.

Yasmiin stood up on shaking legs. Steadied herself. Stretched again. Covered her ringing ears with both hands. She began to hum a song Kari had taught her while they were working on the gelato shop. She didn't know the English words, but the tune had stayed with her. She liked it.

She found a stick. Took the big man's hand. Leaned on the stick until she got her legs under control. She hugged the huge man one final time.

"Merci, Monsieur Jofre."

Yasmiin began making her way home using the stick to steady her walk.

41

The thump of the explosion reached the men in the retreating two-ton. There was elation, but it was joyless. They were down a man, or in this case, a woman. There was nothing more they could do about it.

Mike turned on the walkie-talkie and called Sammy. "Mission accomplished. I'll give you notice when we're on our way."

The groaning two-ton echoed in the background of the walkie-talkie call. Sammy said, "I finally get to hear what's been going on. By the sound of the chatter in the background, I'd say they've been sent to hell."

"And there'll be no coming back. We had to do a bit of manual clean-up, but nothing serious. They're all gone. There is one thing, though. Jofre is missing. We ran circles around the place, but we couldn't find him."

Sammy didn't know what to say. He liked Jofre. He was dependable and knew his stuff.

"I'm sorry to hear that. But there is one more thing—" Sammy released the talk button and hesitated. He pressed it again and went on. "We're going to need three fuel stops. And there's a *Khamsin* on the way."

Mike looked at Harry. Both men shrugged, and Mike pressed the talk button. "What the hell is a Khamsin, Sammy?"

Sammy's voice pitched up a notch. "If you've heard of a ghibli, you know what a Khamsin is." He knew damned well the guys knew what a ghibli was. If they weren't worried before, they would be now. "I suggest you get the lead out. Let me know when you want the engines warmed and ready."

"Roger that. We have two stops to make. Don't leave without us."

No sooner had he said the words than the capitaine's Jeep appeared in front of the two-ton. Harry laid on the horn and the frustrated Jeep driver pulled to the side of the road. Troops disembarked and approached the stopped truck. They called back to the captain to let him know it was Harry and his team.

Harry got out to greet Renaud. He explained how their situation had been resolved, and the captain nodded. "I thought that explosion might be your doing."

"We need to get out of Djibouti." He told the man what he wanted for Kari. He had hoped to spread her ashes from the DC-3, but that would not be possible. "Yasmiin, the girl from the gelato shop, and her mother, will be in contact."

The captain agreed. "My men will want to be there too."

Harry said his goodbyes and thanked the man for his efforts.

"Oh. One more thing, Capitaine. In case there was some doubt, your bomber and his amis are no more. My men will leave their arms on the tarmac at the airport. If you would like to collect them before they fall into the wrong hands."

"Merci bien. Have a safe trip wherever you end up. You can depend on us to take wonderful care of Kari."

In fact, Harry was still processing what had happened to Kari, distraught with grief for the woman he loved. "I would like to stay but—" He couldn't go on.

"It is best if you do not, Harry. The explosion, vous connais."

Harry nodded. "I understand. Au revoir." He climbed into the truck and proceeded to the hotel. He crossed the street to the gelato shop. He met Yasmiin as she too, entered the shop accompanied by the now found Jofre. He gestured for the man to return to the hotel.

When Jofre had gone, Harry said, "Thank you, Yasmiin." He pulled a bundle of dollars out of his pocket and slid them across the counter. "I think you and your mother will know what to do with these."

The girl gave him a forlorn look.

"Capitaine has promised me that Kari will be buried at the Christian Cimetière that is located north of the airport. Do you know of it?"

"Oui. Je connais."

He took out the colorful guntiino, the gift from Bilan and her mother, and handed it to the girl.

She held it up in front of her. "This is very beautiful. I will see that Kari gets it if it is the last thing that I do for her. And for you."

"Thank you. I told the capitaine that you will bring something for her. He will allow you to be present. As for me and Mike and our crew, we must leave the country. It is too dangerous for us to stay any longer."

"I understand. Thank you to you and your men for keeping our secrets."

The men were already waiting in the truck. The engine was running.

"Adieu, ma petite."

He hugged her a final time before climbing in beside Mike. "Airport or bust, driver."

42

The crew arrived to see the DC-3 engines idling, wheel chocks in place to prevent it from moving on the tarmac. Sammy guarded the open cargo door with an AK.

Mike looked at Harry. "Did you radio him?"

"You bet I did, partner. We're not wasting any more time here than we have to."

"Did you tell the men where we're going?"

"Already done. They're coming with us to the last man."

Harry waited until the men were aboard before gravitating to the right seat, allowing Mike to take the left.

Mike nodded. "I know what you're going to do as soon as we become airborne."

"You're right. I'll be going back to pay the men. I shouldn't be long."

Sammy stuck his head past the bulkhead. "There's a Khamsin moving in. We might have eight hours to get out of here, tops."

A Khamsin was a hot, dry and dust-laden sandy wind. It came in the spring. Conditions could last for 50 days, thus the Arabic word for fifty, as it was called. All such winds had their local names. Ghibli, for example, was another, better-known wind. All of them, when conditions were right, were dangerous, especially for an airplane.

"If we get ahead of it, we'll be good. We need three fuel stops. I mapped them out and circled them for the dead reckoners among us. If anything comes up, you know where to find me. I'll be in back with the rest of the rabble. Oh, and Casablanca is two hours behind us time-wise."

Harry radioed the tower to advise that the deux chevaux had been returned to the parking lot. In return, he received departure instructions for Mogadishu, his intended destination per his flight plan.

Mike applied full throttle and the DC-3 lifted off and climbed into the blue sky. He requested an immediate turn, and instructed Harry to look out his window. The cemetery lay off to starboard. A parade of men stood at attention.

"I think I can see little Yasmiin and her mother, Mike."

Mike dipped the wings before dialing in climb power and turning to the west.

Harry raised the gear to two green and called it. "So much for our flight plan and Mog.

Casablanca here we come."

Mike eased back the throttles and leveled at 10,000. He gestured out the front window. "It looks like Sammy was right. We're in for a rough one, partner.

"What the hell else is new, friend? Casablanca or bust, remember?"

Mike unfolded the first of Sammy's charts. "It looks like fifteen hundred nautical to our first stop. Hand me my flight bag, would you, Harry?"

Mike reached into the bag and pulled out his E6B calculator. He began by putting in numbers and coming up with solutions. "We should be able to make the first stop no problem and with fuel to spare. I'm going to feed in some throttle to get us there a little quicker."

Harry pushed back the seat and stood up. "I'm going back to pay the men."

Mike looked up at him. "You are permitted to start without me."

Harry grinned down at Mike, who raised a hand. "Si, mon ami. Have one with the men for me, will you? Oh, and send Sammy back. He knows how to work one of these fancy calculators too. He can check my numbers."

Mike didn't want to slow down Harry's grieving. He knew the man needed to work off his frustrations, and the only way he would do that was with booze. Plenty of booze. The man wasn't needed in the cockpit, anyway.

A tap on Mike's shoulder signaled Sammy's arrival.

Mike waved to the empty first officer seat and Sammy filled it.

Mike passed over the calculator. "Check my numbers, would you? Given what I'm looking at, I don't want to be wrong." He gestured out the window.

In exchange, Sammy handed over the teletype weather reports. They were outdated, but they covered the stations along the North African coast. Some inland stations were included, but they were few and a lot farther between. "Our first will be a piece of cake. I'm not so certain beyond that."

Mike nodded thoughtfully. "We're going to be flying all night for sure. It's a good thing we have lights on the other end. As you said, past that, it's anyone's guess"

Sammy replaced the calculator in Mike's flight bag. "Your numbers are spot-on from what I can tell. Like you said, past that—"

There was silence in the cockpit. Both men knew it would be no piece of cake getting the plane and the men into their final destination through the Khamsin and any following winds.

"How and why did you two pick Casablanca?"

"It's an old Humphrey Bogart movie. I

figured we might as well have a look-see since we're in the neighborhood."

Sammy shook his head. "If you consider 3,000 nautical in the neighborhood, that is."

"Why not? Like Rick said, I stick my neck out for nobody."

"Well, young fella, in that case, you do realize that Casablanca was filmed on the Warner Brothers back lot, right?"

"If that's the case, then we're going for the water."

Sammy shook his head. "There is no water in Casablanca."

Mike shrugged.

Sammy grinned. "Perhaps Bogey or the writers were misinformed." He pushed back the copilot seat and stretched his legs. "Wake me when it's time to lower the gear, Captain."

43

Mike kept the DC-3 ahead of the worst of the Khamsin sandstorm for the first two fuel stops. When he landed for the third, the Khamsin finally caught up to them, thanks to the time on the ground to fill the tanks. He had locked the brakes, but it was all hands on deck to secure the main gear with two sets of wheel chocks. Even so, the tail shuddered and shook on the tail-wheel. It shifted back and forth until Sammy blocked it. He signaled success with a thumbs-up.

It took five men to roll the tallest boarding ramp into position beneath the wing. They fought with the wind all the way. Harry and Mike climbed onto the wing. It took both of them to drag the fueling hose after them. Harry sat down, grabbed a handful of Mike's belt and hung on. When one tank was filled, Mike closed the cap and they crawled to the next. It took them both to drag the fuel into position to repeat the procedure on the starboard wing. When refueling was complete,

Mike closed the cap. He let the hose make its way to the ground on its own while they made their way to the ladder. The pair fought the wind all the way.

"This is our final stop en route Casablanca, Harry. We need to be sure the men dump what's left of their weapons on the tarmac. We won't have another opportunity until we land at Casablanca."

Harry motioned for Jofre and Iván to approach. He let them know about the weapons. "I want you both to keep a couple of sidearms, just in case."

Mike's takeoff took the plane out over the Mediterranean, where he did an immediate 90 degree turn and headed west, climbing all the way. Dust-laden clouds enveloped the DC-3. At 10,000 feet, he reduced climb power and leveled out. He could go no higher if the men were to continue breathing.

Visibility was reduced to almost zero in the sand-laden wind. Mike fought the controls against the gusts and wind-driven dust and sand. Sammy had awoken some time ago. Nervous and exhausted, he was as anxious as Mike was on looking out the window.

"You better go wake the dead, Sammy. I'm pretty sure some of them are going to want to look out and wonder where the hell they are. And send Harry up, drunk or sober."

"I can't say I'm not happy to be leaving the front seat. I'm sick of looking at all that sand. Thanks for everything. I'll see you when you get back. You have my number if you two need anything back home."

Mike nodded. Sammy had obviously already made his decision. He was one of the dependable old-timers who had learned the hard way that being reliable was a feather in his cap. That he could be depended on had made him invaluable to their Africa operation from the very beginning.

"One more thing, Mike. I found this beneath the floor inspection plate." Sammy handed over the oily bag.

Mike opened it and peered inside. "Harry must have put it back."

The grin was all Sammy needed to see. "My job is done. See you on the flyby."

Just as he was thinking Sammy might have spoken too soon, a hungover Harry showed up to take the right seat. "I could smell the fumes in the tank from back there."

"That's the beer you've been drinking while I'm up here busting my ass."

Harry chuckled and looked out the cockpit window. "Where are you planning on landing this tin can?"

The plane shook and groaned through the gusting, sand-laden wind. Mike checked the throttles. He had been mothering the engines every minute since encountering the sandstorm. "I'm descending. Not too slow. Not too fast. Just right for our cargo of bears."

He had dodged some of the storm by flying

farther north. The course change had put him over the Mediterranean. The shoreline was barely visible through the blowing sand. He had reduced throttle. The DC-3 was ever so slowly bound for the ground.

"Night is coming up fast, Harry. We don't have the fuel to make our destination. She's taken us as far as she's going to. The last thing I want is to run out of fuel in the dark and in the air. I need to get her on the ground. Dead reckoning tells me we're going to be 40 or 50 miles from Casablanca."

Harry looked out the starboard cockpit window. "I think I can see Spain from here. What's your problem?"

The port engine coughed. Mike checked the gauges. As if to confirm his suspicion, the engine backfired. He fed in mixture, but the engine finally quit. There was no fuel remaining in the port tank. "That's my problem. Fuel starvation on number one. I'm calling for a straight in. What do you think, First Officer Delaney?"

Harry got up out of his seat. "You know, running out of fuel in the air is a firing offense in my book."

Mike swiped at his sweat-laden brow. "It is in mine too." He looked out the window at the all-enveloping dark and grinned. "But since this is a fly-by-night operation, I think I'm in the clear on that one."

Harry stepped past the doorway.

"Where the hell are you going just when I need a First Officer?

"I'll be right back. I'm going to warn the men to brace. We can work the rest out after we land. Have you got Kari's camera?"

Mike nodded, and Harry fished it out of Mike's flight bag. He inserted a cube and aimed through the bulkhead and into the cargo hold. To a man, they smiled broadly. All of them were still wearing the Hawaiian shirts.

Mike fed in mixture for number two. He kicked in rudder and fought with the controls in an effort keep the DC-3 as steady and straight as he could in the gusting wind. Ever so slowly, he eased back the throttle on number two and checked the altimeter. It continued to unwind to confirm proximity to the ground. His course was still over the Mediterranean. The shoreline became slightly more visible. "I might get us out of this yet."

Harry slapped him on the back. "Who you talking to, partner?"

"Nice to see you up front to be first on the scene of the accident with me. Give me some gear, would you? I've only got two hands."

Mike flipped the landing light to *On*. A huge rock cliff appeared to port. "Si, mon capitaine.

Harry called out *Two green*. It was only then that he noticed the rock cliff to port. "Holy shit. Turn off that light. You're scaring me."

Mike fought the gusting wind to ease the DC-3

into a gentle bump onto the beach. The gusting wind died all of a sudden. The plane dropped. The gentle bump turned into a loud bang as the gear smashed into the water-soaked beach. It bounced, and the gear slammed onto the beach a second time. Still fighting, Mike yanked back the throttle on number two and kicked rudder to compensate.

The plane settled onto the sand. The gear caught. The nose pitched down. The tail came up. At the last minute, a gust leveled it and the tail bumped gently onto the beach. The starboard engine died. "Call for a fuel bowser, would you, Harry? You can pay with these." Mike handed over the bag of uncut gemstones.

"You better go check on our passengers. They'll be wondering where we are."

Harry was wondering too, until Mike read his mind. "About 40 miles east of Casablanca. A good day's march for the guys. Not so good for you and me."

Harry waved the bag. "This should get us there in jig time, Captain."

44

The wind had died. The tide was coming in. Water began lapping at the landing gear. The DC-3 had turned when it hit the ground. The nose faced the shore.

Jofre opened the cargo door. Sunlight flooded into the back of the plane. "Nous sommes arrivés." Already he had taken a bearing. He grabbed a shovel and dug a shallow hole in the sand. It filled immediately with water.

"Drop the sidearms into the pit. We are not in friendly territory if we are caught."

An invisible truck groaned, hidden behind a sand dune.

"By the sound of it we're not going to have to march."

The men made their way over the crest of the dune. A highway partially obscured by sand greeted them. Vehicle trails met and divided and met again in the new sand covering parts of the roadway.

"We are in luck. Casablanca, here we come."

The men didn't walk for long. A passing one-ton groaning its way west over the sand-obscured highway halted. The driver shouted. "Casablanca?"

"Si. Aéroport."

One-way fares bought and paid for, the comrades in arms bid farewell. It was the last Harry saw of the men, but for his picture of them in the back of the DC-3, sporting broad smiles and wearing Kari's Hawaiian shirts.

Epilogue

Harry **turned over** the photo of the men in the back of the DC-3 and handed it to Sasha. "That was our crew. Two squads. Ten good men. Led by the best of the best, Iván and Jofre." He pointed out the two men, looking proud in their shirts. The very shirts Kari had chosen for them. "Jofre was Catalan. A damn good squad leader. Iván too."

Sasha handed the photo across the table to Christa.

The girl took one look at the brightly colored shirts. "Dad, why are they all wearing Hawaiian shirts? I thought you guys were going to Casablanca. I don't think anyone wears those kinds of shirts there."

"Perhaps we were misinformed." Harry looked at Sasha and they both grinned. "That was their way of paying tribute to Kari. Jofre took it particularly hard after she manned up the comms during his firefight. She thought Mike was radioing to tell her he was on fire. It took her a minute or two to realize that he was *under* fire. And then she ran to chase us up and let us know. After that, she was special to all of us."

Sasha reached for Harry's hand and took it in her own.

Christa continued to study the photo. "They're all in an airplane. Are we going back to Africa, dad?"

Harry sighed. "No, dear. Africa is in our past. Even yours, remember?"

"I remember you and Uncle Mike had to come and get us. I was pretty glad to see you, too, wasn't I, Mom?"

"We both were, dear. We both were."

Christa picked up the passport and opened it to Kari's picture. "She was pretty. Not as pretty as Mom, but almost."

"That was long before I met your father, dear. I'm sure he knew lots of girls that were almost as pretty as me. But you're right. She is beautiful." Sasha smiled at Harry.

Christa looked to her father. "Did she stay in Africa, Dad?"

Harry let out a long sigh. "Yes. Karita stayed in Africa. She's in Djibouti to this very day."

Christa thought for a moment. "Djibouti? Isn't that where me and Mom met up with Uncle Mike?"

"That's right."

"So we won't have to go to Djibouti and rescue Kari?"

Harry looked at his daughter and smiled. "No, dear. We don't have to go and rescue Karita."

Christa pushed back her chair, hugged her mother and father, and skipped away to climb the stairs to her room.

Her mother moved to follow her.

"Wait a minute, Sasha. You need to know something about this weapon. It's very important. Come and I'll show you."

Check out all six books of the Harry Delaney Adventure series. Learn why Harry makes his way from the North African desert to the Mexican Baja. Discover why he ends up having a triumphal return to the deserts of North Africa.

Print books

Jim Nash
Jim Nash The Beginning
Gun Crazy
Gun Crazy 2
Gun Crazy 3
Fallen Angels
Last Stop to Nowhere
Revenge is Justice
Escape / Forget Me Not
Wedding Bell Blues / Breakdown
Mexico Time
No Free Ride / Gone
LOBO
Stealing America
Blame It on Djibouti
No Escape
Trouble in Paradise
Nash & Delaney Collide

Harry Delaney Adventures
Dead Reckoning
Lie Cheat Steal
Uncharted
Go-Around
Sand Storm
Harry Delaney Collection

Frank Ross Biker Tales
No Way Out
Bad Girls
Bank Robber Dames

Other
The Last President

<h1 style="text-align:center">Jim Nash Read Order</h1>

<table>
<tr><td valign="top" width="50%">

JIM NASH

Jim Nash The Beginning
Pirate Cay
Thrill Kill Jill
Greetings From Key West
Lost Paradise
No Angels
Mexico Gamble
No Picnic
Fallen Angels
Vendetta
A Girl's Best Friend
Dead End
No Harbor
Dog Days
Startup Blues
Last Stop To Nowhere / The Last
Goodbye
Revenge Is Justice
Escape
Wedding Bell Blues
Snap Brim Fedora Caper
Breakdown
Little Girl Lost
Forget Me Not
All The Glitter
Mexico Time
Partners In Crime
Shop Till You Drop
Lobo
No Free Ride
Gone
Stealing America
Blame It on Djibouti
No Escape
Trouble in Paradise
Nash & Delaney Collide

</td><td valign="top" width="50%">

SEASONAL

Trick or Treat
Helping Santa

JIM NASH INVESTIGATES

The Snap Brim Fedora Caper
The Lady in White
The Lady in Yellow

</td></tr>
</table>

PX DUKE
JIM NASH
00
THE BEGINNING

www.ingramcontent.com/pod-product-compliance
Lightning Source LLC
Chambersburg PA
CBHW011556190726
48287CB00010B/2914